AFTER THE WAR:

TWO TALES OF NOREELA

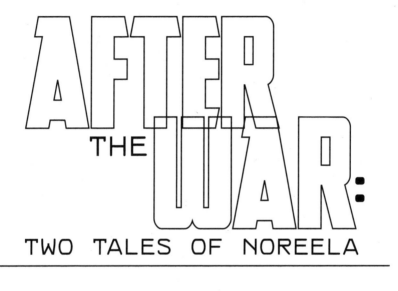

AFTER THE WAR:
TWO TALES OF NOREELA

TIM LEBBON

Subterranean Press 2008

First Edition

ISBN
978-1-59606-139-2

Subterranean Press
PO Box 190106
Burton, MI 48519

www.subterraneanpress.com

For Deena, my Web-Angel

INTRODUCTION

I USED to think that writers create a new world every time they set pen to paper. The story or novel may be set here and now, but the world is distinctly that of the writer and no one else. Things often happen here that would never occur elsewhere. It's unique. I used to think that, at least.

Then I started writing a fantasy novel.

Talk about a whole new world!

THE IMAGINARY world of Noreela—setting for my novels *Dusk* and *Dawn*, the forthcoming *Fallen* and *The Island*, and the novellas "The Bajuman" and "Vale of Blood Roses" contained herein—is the first time I've created a whole new world. Its genesis lies in a throwaway remark from a work colleague about ten years ago. At the time I was writing short stories for some of the wonderful small press magazines in the UK with such intriguing names as *Psychotrope*, *Peeping Tom*, *Grotesque* and *Dreams from the Stranger's Café*, and I was also working on my first novel. My good friends where I worked knew about what I did, and most of them were very supportive (I say most, because there's always one, isn't there? In my case that "one" was an ex-boss who, upon reading one of my stories, said, "Why don't you write something normal, like Wilbur Smith?" I killed that boss in *The Nature of Balance*. Squashed him flat. There's normal for you). Other people in work I didn't mix with so much still had an inkling, and one day in the tea room a colleague asked exactly what I wrote.

"Horror and dark fantasy," I said.

"Right. Skull fucking and magic swords, yeah?"

No, I thought, but to my best recollection I did not reply.

Back at my desk I thought about the "magic" part of what he'd said. I considered that writing about magic was mainly the job of fantasy writers, and that led me to challenge myself to dream up my own fantasy world (it was a slow day, perhaps I had a hangover, and it was sunny and bright outside... *not* a day for work). Now, before I go on I should tell you that back then I had an office job, working in the Building department of a Local Authority. I was in control of the financial and contractual side of building projects—schools, leisure centres, retirement homes. It was not thrilling. But I was lucky enough to sit at a desk with a panoramic view across the local town and the hills that surround it, and I'll admit that I spent some time whilst employed staring out at this view, dreaming...

So, back to my challenge. My own fantasy world. I'd not read much fantasy back then—*The Lord of the Rings*, a bit of Gemmell—and rightly or wrongly I believed then that the bulk of fantasy novels had magic at their core: magic crystals, swords or people, talking dragons, elves and witches delving into arcane matters. So I stared out at that glorious view and imagined it all as a place none of us really knew. There could be castles and shimmering waterfalls, but that felt all wrong. It felt like the covers of fantasy novels I saw in the local bookshop, and I wanted something different. So I rubbed those castles from my imagination... but not all the way. Their ruins remained. And I was onto something.

I wondered how fascinating it could be to write in an alternate world that once had magic, but from which that magic had been taken away. I started making notes (which happened quite regularly at work... indeed, I'd often come home with a spray of blue and yellow Post-its sticking from my top pocket like a fake handkerchief). Later, as I switched off my computer to go home, a perfect analogy hit me: imagine our world if electricity suddenly stopped working. Perhaps caused by a cataclysm, or a sudden and inexplicable shift in all the laws of physics we think we know. No more electricity.

Pause. Think about that for a bit.

Jump forward several years. I'd had some books published by now—novellas, collections and a couple of novels—and I was feeling more capable of tackling this fantasy story that had been slowly developing in my mind for years. It often reared its head, and I'd amassed a small pile of notes about what this world would be like. But I'd done no serious work on it, other than the occasional daydream about the form such a story could take.

And then I was asked by a publisher who'd heard about this idea to show them some sample chapters. Once I started writing *Dusk* I couldn't stop. Noreela was born. But I had no idea what I'd bitten off.

THIS REALLY was a *whole new world*!

I drew a map. I'd always wanted a book with a map, and I made casual, spontaneous decisions that would have an effect on some of the stories I came to tell. I didn't feel it at the time, but what I was doing was more God-like than anything I'd ever done before. I was *designing* this new world—a massive island, though I'm not sure where that idea came from—and where I pencilled in mountain ranges, inland seas, forests, cities and surrounding islands actually informed much of the tales I would come to tell about this world. It didn't feel restrictive in any way, and in fact I think seeing the place where these stories were taking place helped focus my thoughts.

A bit of card, a pencil, some made-up names (and more about those in a minute), and Noreela was there before me. I looked at one mountain range and wondered who lived there, how they survived and what creatures and things they had to contend with. I looked at The Spine, the string of islands I had brought into being north of mainland Noreela, and tried to picture how individual islands would trade or fight. There was an area to the south of Noreela which was still vague in my mind, and that became The Blurring, a place unknown to Noreelans. Perhaps in the future they'll find out some more about it, but they'll have to wait until I've been there first.

Noreela was starting to feel real and now, maybe 6 years on, the more I write about it, the more authentic it feels. Weird. I'll never go there—not physically, at least—but it's far more familiar to me than many places I've never visited in this "real" world of ours. I know more about Noreela than I do about Chile.

And naming this new world? That was easy. I started writing *Dusk* just about the time we had our first child. We called her Eleanor. And so my made-up world, set to become the most important place I'd ever written about, became Noreela.

INTRODUCTION

AS I wrote *Dusk* and *Dawn* I realised how much more there was to know. Being a writer, and endlessly curious, this excited me a great deal.

Writing the first two novels was a labour of love unlike any I had experienced in my writing before, and as I created and dreamed up new places, people, religions, societies, landscapes, history, drugs, foods, animals and plants, I realised that this was not only a place I *could* visit again and again, but a place I *wanted* to return to. The Noreela I wrote about was grim, dark and in pain, but the world drew me in a very strange way. It started to feel like a real place, and I wanted to know more of its history. I'm exploring its distant past in my new novel *Fallen*. And the two novellas in this volume are also a part of that expanded history.

The first novella in this volume is very recent. I'm currently finishing up my third novel set in Noreela, *Fallen*, which is set four thousand years before the Cataclysmic War. Yet when Subterranean Press head honcho Bill Schafer asked me to write a new novella set in this world, I found myself returning yet again to that war and its terrible aftermath. The result is "Vale of Blood Roses".

For Noreela, the Cataclysmic War was worse in many ways than the World Wars we have experienced. The death and destruction was terrible but it resulted in a very fundamental change in Noreela—the withdrawal of magic—and it was that more than the brutality of the war that doomed the land to its terrible decline. In a way, *Dusk* and *Dawn* together tell a post-apocalyptic story set in a fantasy land, and I'm sure this is a setting I'll return to again and again.

In "Vale of Blood Roses", dead machines litter the landscape. The story follows a small band of mercenaries as they make their way north. They've been under the employ of the Ventgorians, fighting against the Soyaran who have used the Cataclysmic War as cover under which to attack from the Poison Forests. The battles these mercenaries have fought, and the terrible things they have done, are in the past. The novella concerns the strange place they find on their journey home and what happens there. And in the future—the later strand of the novella—they reap what they have sown.

The second novella was written at the beginning of 2006. When *Dusk* was released in January of that year I started a website at www.noreela.com, run by the supremely talented Deena Warner (and if you ever need a website designed I'd recommend Deena wholeheartedly). I wanted a place separate from my general website where people could go and find out more about Noreela. I invited artists to illustrate scenes from the book, and on Noreela.com you'll find a varied gallery of images. I also created a reference page where I talked about all manner of things, from characters in the books to the things they ate and drank. About this time I had an idea for a shorter tale set in Noreela City itself, called "The Bajuman", and I decided to serialise it on the site as it was written.

"The Bajuman" is a detective story told against the backdrop of a Noreela City in decline. It's set one hundred years before *Dusk*, two hundred years after the Cataclysmic War resulted in magic being withdrawn from the land. It also follows an event I alluded to in *Dusk*, the Great Plagues. I guess in a way it's noir fantasy. I wanted to make my main character—the narrator, Korrin—more than just a detective (in the novella he calls himself a hunter). And so he became the Bajuman of the title, a Noreelan equivalent of the untouchables of India, shunned by most because of some unexplained, ambiguous wrongdoing in the mists of history. This is prejudice of the first order, and if most people don't actually hate the Bajuman, they are generally ignored. Who better to be a detective than someone who can hide in plain view?

It's dark, gritty and grim, both the story and its setting. This is a world where a race of people were once bred solely for food, and even though that was centuries in the past and the fodder are now a part of society... well, some people still have exotic tastes. When a fodder is kidnapped, it's up to Korrin to find him before he falls victim to these tastes.

I HOPE you enjoy these two novellas. I hope they encourage you to visit Noreela again. And I hope you're as excited about this strange world as I am.

I can't get Noreela out of my head. There's so much more to know, and I'm doing my best to discover. The new novel *Fallen* features two Voyagers exploring parts of Noreela not yet known. I feel a bit like a Voyager as well, only I'm much luckier than they are. Because I can travel in time.

I want to know more about The Blurring, the Sleeping Gods, the living-dead Violet Dogs, the strange and alluring Cantrass Angels and those who choose to dwell within the Poison Forests. Fingers crossed I'll have the opportunity to find out. ◦⌒

Tim Lebbon
Goytre
June 2007

VALE OF
BLOOD ROSES

THERE IS a smell in the air as he throws stones at the skull ravens, and he has smelled it before, and recurring nightmares come back at him like yet more of those vicious birds, pecking and probing and doing their utmost to undo his mind. Jakk Young pauses with one stone remaining in his hand and three ravens in the tree. The odds excite him. The creatures watch him with their soulless eyes, and soon they will call back their brethren he has scared off.

He sniffs, throws the stone and watches the final three birds fly away. Even then it feels as though they are laughing at him. He sniffs again, taking slow, measured breaths. He turns around slowly, scanning the woods for any sign of movement. But there is nothing, and he is alone. The smell has vanished now—if it was ever there at all—and those briefly recalled nightmares are beyond his grasp once more. But the memories, though faded and sometimes so remote that they feel like the recollections of others, are always there.

Jakk gathers his backpack, bow and the ground squirrel he shot earlier and starts for home. The woods have come alive again now that he has seen away the skull ravens, and the canopy sings with the busy, complex concert of Pengulfin Woods' wildlife. Wood sparks grind their legs to scratch out their mating calls. Song birds try to outdo each other in range, volume and beauty. Ochre tree frogs groan and growl, lizards whisper their way across rough bark and crown ants whistle softly as they expel venom into the guts of their unfortunate prey. Noises he knows and is familiar with, and they make Jakk feel at home. He knows the geography of this part of the forest so well that he could walk this final mile with his eyes closed. The noises and smells make shapes, locating tree and path, rock and stream. He has been here for fifteen years, yet it is only recently that he started to understand the language of the land.

A hundred steps further on, he knows that something is wrong.

That smell, he thinks. It came back like the ghost of a memory, not smelled but remembered; caked dust, blood-roses trampled underfoot, death in waiting. He knows it is bad, but his memories are in turmoil, fighting and rolling with nightmares so that he is not quite sure which are which. The idea that he could have lost so many bad memories is, in a way, worse than being able to remember them all. They stalk him, unknown and hidden away. Even after so long, he knows that dangers you can see and understand are much less terrible than horrors you cannot.

He is suddenly eager to reach home. He enjoys hunting in the woods, welcomes time on his own away from Bindy and their child Romana, but now he wishes nothing more than to be with them again. The frogs' calls are mocking, the wood sparks do not bode well. And as he crests the small rise to the east of their homestead in a clearing in the woods, and that smell from the past is real once again, he sees that one of his nightmares is about to make itself known.

HIS DAUGHTER Romana stands at the entrance to their humble home, one hand holding the door half-open behind her, the other pressed to her mouth as if to hold in a cry. It's not like Romana to be so quiet, and Jakk knows that she is shocked, upset or afraid. Perhaps all three.

Bindy is a dozen steps from the timber building, kneeling beside a shape splayed on the ground. The shape is a man. Jakk's wife seems frozen above him, one hand outstretched but unable to touch whoever it is.

That's where the smell is coming from, Jakk thinks. *That shape. That person. Blood roses rotting, and he must have come here to return my nightmares to me.*

Bindy looks back at the building. "Roma, bring water, quickly."

"Mother...?"

"Water, Roma. And see if you can find the horn. We need your father here."

For a few beats Jakk feels like an intruder, viewing a scene he was never meant to see. *They don't know I'm here,* he thinks, and for a few beats more he remains motionless and silent, watching his wife's naturally caring soul fighting and debating what to do, how to touch.

What must she be seeing? That stink is bad, and it would be amazing if the person is not already dead.

"No need for the horn," he says at last. The relief on Bindy's face is a comfort, but also a warning.

"Jakk, thank the Black! He stumbled in, collapsed, and I think he might be—"

"Don't touch," Jakk says. He hurries down the gentle slope, keeping to the path they have worn here over the years. He knows the route so well that he does not need to look, and that way he can examine the man sprawled on the ground before his wife.

Dead, Bindy wants to say. *I think he might be dead.* But Romana is still watching from the doorway and listening to her parents' conversation. A growing girl, death is becoming something of a preoccupation. The fact that Jakk refuses to talk about it perhaps makes it worse, but he has seen too much death to be able to discuss it with his daughter. Every question she asks dredges up bad memories.

And Old Parkgan doesn't help, wandering through the forest and telling anyone who will listen that the Cataclysmic War has marked the end. *Borrowed time*, he says. *We're all inhaling the land's final breath.*

As if to prove everyone wrong, the prone man groans.

"Roma, hurry with that—"

He shouts, sits up and reaches for Bindy. She falls back and kicks out, knocking his hand aside and scurrying backwards on hands and feet.

"Bindy!" Jakk drops the dead ground squirrel and bow and runs, pulling his knife as he does so. It whispers against the leather scabbard, and his blood is suddenly on fire.

"Jakk!" the man says when he looks around. "Jakk Young!"

Jakk pauses a dozen steps away, hand still clasping the knife's handle. The man has dark skin. No hair, a bulky body that may have once been strong. To begin with Jakk does not know him, because he has changed so much. But he can smell him. And he can see the blossoming blood roses on the man's stomach, spread in a splash as though planted there with a flourish. "No," Jakk says. "I don't know you."

The man laughs. It sounds mad. "But you know these, Jakk?" He runs his hand across the tops of the stubby flowers, and fleshy petals kiss at his fingertips. "And you know you can't *forget* what we did, can't just *shut it away!*"

"Roma, that water, now," Jakk says. She disappears inside and closes the door behind her.

"It's come," the man says.

"What's come?"

"Revenge…like we always knew it would." The man raises himself on both arms, stretching forward as if to take a bite from the air. "Jakk, I only just got away! They've already got Rufiere and Leeza, and I only just…."He touches the blooming things across his stomach again, and below them Jakk can now see a deep, ugly cut. Things protrude from there, and they look like coiled grey guts. "But I didn't get away for long. I cut one, it bled, and now…."

Jakk feels cold. *Revenge*, the man said. And those nightmares are circling, coalescing, and Jakk can hear them mocking him from where he thought he had buried them away. "Stay away from my family," he says quietly.

"You have to get away!"

"Stay down. Don't get up." He walks backwards to where he dropped the bow, picks it up and strings an arrow. He does not take his eyes from the sick man, not for an instant. That would be dangerous.

"Jakk?" Bindy says. "Who is he? What's wrong with him?"

"Haven't you told her anything?" the man asks. He laughs but there's little humour there, only disbelief. "Nothing at all?"

Jakk sights along the arrow. *Shut up*, he thinks, *shut up, shut up, please give me any excuse and I'll* make *you shut up.*

"Ventgoria," the man says. "Jakk and I fought the Soyaran from the Poison Forests."

"Jakk fought the Krotes in the Cataclysmic War," Bindy says, but she's looking at Jakk now more than the man.

Jakk stares back. He blinks slowly. *I'll tell you soon*, he tries to convey. *I lied, and I'll tell you soon. But not right now.*

"It's come for us," the man says again. "The heart and mind." He spits out a mouthful of blood.

Jakk breathes in deeply and wonders when his turn will come.

———

THE VALLEY was not meant to be there, so that's why they went in. It appeared before them as they marched north out of the bloodied borderlands between Ventgoria and the Poison Forests. Behind them they had left a field of dead bodies, piled three deep and burning. The southerly breeze gusted the stench of cooking meat after them, the smell of guilt having little effect on these people. They had left any morals at home years ago. Remorse had no place in their new world of blood and money.

Barr wore a necklace of thumbs sliced from his victims, one from each. At least forty were strung around his neck. Jakk had told him how foolish he was being; there was no trusting the blood of the Poison Forest tribes. But Barr had started collecting these gruesome trophies at the beginning of their campaign, and none of them had sickened him yet. Jakk knew that Barr had an immortality complex, with knife wounds, acid spit burns and a badly-healed slashed throat testament to his claim. Jakk also knew that when such men fell, they fell hard.

The others—only four remained from their original force of twenty—marked kills in their own unique ways. Rufiere kept shreds of cloth from his victims' clothing, and he was making himself a ragged coat of many colours and textures. Leeza cut her arm every time she killed, and her left arm was a scarred map of victories. They held various other mementoes, medals of success and marks of triumph... but Jakk kept nothing. He was not here to keep score, a tally to boast of later in life over mugs of rotwine around camp fires. He knew the face of every man, woman and child he had killed, and sometimes at night they smiled at him.

"What in the Black is that?" Rufiere said. He claimed he had a Book of Ways, and though the others knew him as a liar, they grudgingly admitted that he always found the most favourable routes from one place to the next. "Shouldn't be here. This is woodland and grassland, a few marshes, all the way north to the Cantrass Plains. No valleys. *Nothing* like this."

"Obviously your little book's wrong," Barr said.

They had topped a small crest and now a narrow valley lay before them. It was a deep, almost brutal wound in the land, its sides a mixture of sheer cliffs, shale slopes and rocky promontories, with only a few seemingly manageable routes down into its depths. It ran south to north, its southernmost reach before them now. Sunlight fought to illuminate its depths, but clouds to the north and a heavy yellow mist closer by sought to deny the sun access. It gave the valley the appearance of somewhere that did not belong.

Rufiere pulled the small battered leather-bound book from his jacket pocket and made a show of consulting several pages. "A way north," he said. "That's what should be here. Look, double-humped hill to the east, flatter ground to the west with a forest a few miles distant. And here...." He pointed ahead at the rift in the ground. "Here, an easy route north. Streams to drink from, terrain not too difficult to cross."

"Looks difficult as fuckery to me." Barr took a lump of harshroot from his pocket and bit off a chunk, chewed, grimaced past the initial bitterness to the alluring sweetness beneath.

"We should take a look," Jakk said.

"Listen!" Leeza hissed. She rarely spoke, and when she did her voice, with its exotic southern accent and deep seriousness, sounded unused.

They all listened and Jakk heard the sound immediately. Heard it, but did not quite believe. "Machines?" he said.

"No," Rufiere said. "Can't be."

"Why not?" asked Barr, inviting argument.

"Because all the machines are dead." Jakk stepped forward to distance himself from his mercenary companions, trying to decide exactly what he was hearing. Grinding, clanking, the sound of venting steam and sighing heat, wheels whispering over loose stones....

"There!" he said. *Machines!* He could hardly believe it. The machines had died three years before at the end of the Cataclysmic War, and since that shock the land had been suffering a steady regression towards more basic times. Now, in this valley that should not exist, he could see three machines working the hillside, plucking short purple plants from the ground, dropping them into fleshy hoppers on their backs and venting shredded greenery into the air behind them.

Jakk had forgotten how beautiful they were. Their movements were smooth and graceful. Their fuel was magic.

And magic was no more.

"This is not real," Jakk said.

"Looks real enough to me." Barr was the first of them to step across the obvious boundary between the land that should be there and the valley that should not.

For an instant Jakk expected something to happen to him. He would disappear, collapse or be destroyed because of his trespass. Jakk held his breath and watched his fighting companion start down the slope. Barr paused after a few steps and raised his face to the sky, and Jakk thought, *This is when it happens.* But he had seen enough corpses to know that he was far from dead.

"Smells good," Barr said. "Smells like blood. Coming?"

The machines worked away to their left, lower down the slopes and deeper into the valley. They seemed to not notice Barr's invasion into their territory.

The others followed Barr, and Jakk followed them. *Perhaps I've seen enough of blood,* he thought. But he had long ago stopped trying to deny his true nature. The idea of a fight drew him on, and the mention of blood set his own on fire.

The possibility of slaughter had not yet entered his mind.

———

THE WOMAN was walking slowly across the hillside, stepping carefully between sprouting heathers and looking down at her feet. She carried a soft bag in one hand and a squat metallic device in the other, the two connected by a thin flexible tube. Every few steps she paused and worked the device in her right hand, expelling a few droplets of red fluid onto the ground. She waited as if to watch the drops soak in, then moved on. Behind her, marking the path she had taken, thin red shoots were already peering between blades of grass.

She's beautiful, thought Jakk. He was more used to the infected, scarred Soyaran women of the Poison Forests, and seeing this woman's smooth pale skin and raven hair was a shock.

She looked up as they approached, and for a beat her expression did not register anything, almost as if it took her a few moments to see them. Then she stumbled back with a cry and fell over.

"Wait!" Jakk said. He moved forward, hands held out. "We're not here to hurt you." *Then why are we here?* he thought, *if hurting is what we do best?*

The woman crawled back, her face an image of terror. She had dropped the bag and dripping device and they leaked into the ground. *Maybe it's the weapons,* Jakk thought. *Or our sudden appearance from out of the valley. Maybe she's the only one here.*

Jakk reached for his bow and slipped it from his shoulder. The woman screamed again.

"Who are you?" he asked. The question felt foolish, but she spoke words that made no sense, garbled noises that conveyed only fear and upset.

"Just another tribe," Barr said.

"No, she doesn't recognise us, doesn't think—"

"Tell us who you are!" Rufiere shouted. "You shouldn't even be here. You're not in the book, you're not *here!*"

Still the woman screamed, and Jakk saw that she was looking at their weapons; the bow in his hand, the sword and knives strapped to his belt.

He heard the whistle of the arrow at the same instant it embedded itself in the woman's throat.

"No!" Jakk shouted.

Barr laughed. Leeza scolded him half-heartedly. Rufiere sighed and shook his head, looking down at the book that lied.

The woman lay on her back, hands clawing at her throat as blood began pulsing from the wound.

Jakk ran, careful to step over the bag she had dropped. By the time he reached her the woman had stopped moving, and he saw the life go from her eyes.

"Why did you do that?" he shouted, turning to Barr.

"Way she talked, she's just another—"

"She looks *nothing like* the Soyaran!"

"Well, maybe not her face. But—"

"But nothing. We're finished here. The Ventgorians don't want our help anymore, Barr, and the killing is over."

"Jakk?" Leeza said, and she seemed genuinely confused.

He looked at her, at Rufiere, and when Barr drew his knife and walked past him to the dead woman Jakk turned to stare down into the valley. He heard clothes ripping, Barr grunting and sighing, and then the crunch of her thumb bone breaking as he took his trophy.

I really believed it had all ended, he thought. And then the smell of fresh blood wafted up from the depths of the valley, and he knew that they were somewhere special.

———

"BARR," JAKK says.

Barr looks up and coughs more bloody mess. He smiles a red smile. He knows that Jakk would never have forgotten him.

I could kill him now, Jakk thinks. *Slit his throat while he's puking. Let it flow for real.* But he has not killed anyone for fifteen years, not since the folded valley opened itself to them.

Barr's smile widens, strings of vomit hanging from his nose, blood speckling his cheeks. He spits and wipes the mess from his lips. "I knew you'd never forget," he says. Though his voice contains a triumphant lilt, there is nothing of hope in him. Jakk can see that the man in dying, and he knows it very well.

"Barr," Jakk says again.

"Who is he?" Bindy asks.

"Someone I thought was dead."

"You know I'm stronger," Barr says. "You know it takes a lot to kill—"

"Someone I *wished* was dead." Jakk raises the bow again. The gut creaks as he pulls back, a sound that fills the clearing in the forest that he calls home. Livestock grow still, birds' singing fades, chickens stop pecking at the ground. Jakk remembers the woman dropping those fluid seeds, how Barr had killed her and what he did to her after she was dead. He'd seen that many times before—especially from Barr—but this first dead woman of the folded valley stuck in his mind. He supposes it was the first truly innocent death he had seen.

"Won't be long now," Barr says. He has stopped vomiting and he sits up, moving slowly as if every move pains him. "They've killed Rufiere and Leeza, and two moons ago they came for me. I got away, but...." He indicates his stomach where the blood roses bloom. "Soon, they'll come for you."

"Daddy?" Romana says. She is standing at the door to their home, a jug of water slowly tipping in her left hand and darkening the front of her dress.

"Stay back," Jakk says.

"But...." She is looking at Barr's injuries and what grows there, and the bloody mess on the ground beside him. Jakk wonders what she makes of this man's drawn, haunted expression. Haunted, even through his grin.

"They'll die too," Barr says. He nods at Romana and she drops the jug. "Her. And the woman. They'll kill them too, and they won't be as lucky as me. You should hear what they did to Rufiere. How he screamed. How he begged."

"The woman is my wife," Jakk says. "Don't you even look at her."

"Remembering more now, Jakk?" Barr stares at Bindy, very obviously looking her up and down.

"Enough."

"Jakk?" Bindy says. Jakk can hear the fear beneath her voice and he goes to her, keeping the arrow trained on the wounded man.

"Enough to know you won't escape?" Barr asks. "You must know that."

"Then why come to me?"

"Because I'm twisted."

"You're talking shit."

"Enough to realise you were just as bad? We were all just as bad, Jakk. It's just that some of us lived with it, while others fought against it. And lost. Fight it and you *always* lose."

Jakk has the sudden feeling that Barr is not only talking to them. He looks around, and there is no one visible through the trees, no hint that they are being watched. But he can suddenly smell those blood roses again, and the scent is so much sweeter than that rising from this man's death-vomit, the blossoms on his stomach, the redness seeping from their leaves. His rush of memory solidifies some more.

"I was not as bad as you," Jakk says.

Barr laughs, a wet croak. "You always knew what you wanted, you were just never strong enough—"

"I was nowhere *near* as bad!"

"Jakk, what's happening?" Bindy says, and Jakk can see that she is glancing around the clearing as well. *Because she saw me doing it?* he wonders. *Or can she sense something as well?*

"In the house," he says, and Bindy knows the gravity in his voice.

27

"Romana." Bindy ushers their daughter inside, but the door does not close. She is watching her husband.

"I came to warn you," Barr says. He coughs another spurt of blood, dark and rancid.

"Why?" At the edges of his perception more of those nightmares dance, memories stalking him like wolves probing a field of sheebok.

"We were brothers," Barr says quietly.

"No."

"Brothers of the sword, the knife, the bolt." Barr spits and groans, pressing one hand to the roses sprouting across his stomach. They seem to envelop his hand, curling and stretching to cover his skin.

"What has come?" Jakk asks.

"The ghosts. Ghosts of the folded valley. Come for us."

"What killed Rufiere and Leeza?"

"I just told you! What we did killed them. The heart and mind has come for us at last, and—"

"*You* did it, not me. It was over for me by then." Jakk still holds the bow, aim never wavering. He has seen Barr's tricks before, knows him too well.

Romana whispers something behind him, but Bindy hisses something in response.

"I'm dying," Barr says.

"Good."

"Maybe you can...."

"I can what?" Jakk is becoming impatient, eyes flickering around the clearing as he senses something not only watching him, but marking him, *knowing* him.

"Make amends." Barr grins again, and Jakk can no longer see the bleeding, wounded, dying man. He sees the warrior that was—a murderer by any other name—and the chord of severed thumbs he wore around his neck. And he remembers more of what that warrior-murderer did in the valley they unfolded.

Jakk blinks slowly, then fires the arrow into Barr's chest. The dying man gasps in surprise, and it is the last sound he makes.

"Jakk!" Bindy shouts. The door slams shut.

I can't hear Romana, Jakk thinks. *If she saw, she'd have screamed. If she saw what I did, I'd have heard her by now.*

Barr writhes on the ground for a few beats, hands pressing around the arrow but never actually touching it. He blinks rapidly at Jakk, eyelids moving slower, and then finally they, and he are still.

"If making amends is the only way, then that's a good beginning." Jakk turns away without another glance and walks to the house. He must prepare his family to leave.

———

HE COULD have turned around and walked out of the valley. After all they had been through—fighting for the Ventgorians, losing comrades and friends to the Soyaran raiders from the Poison Forests, hearing of the Cataclysmic War and feeling the impact of its culmination reverberating through the land—Jakk should have known what to expect. He had known Barr well enough by then to understand.

But he did not turn around. Part of the reason was the companionship he felt for these survivors with whom he had been fighting for the past several years. He did not particularly like them, but each of them had been saved by the others many times over. The more they killed, the more precious their own lives became, and they owed each other everything. And another reason was a fascination with what the valley might contain, and the simple fact that it should not have been here at all.

Machines! They had heard that the machines were dead all across Noreela. They had seen many of them themselves, already rusting and rotting down into the land wherever they had come to a halt. The thought of life going on without them was dreadful and difficult to comprehend. Jakk had felt more than most of them the sickening, gut-twisting hollowness of magic fading from Noreela at the end of the war, so the prospect of seeing it at work again was something he could not miss.

And yet, looking back at the dead, raped, mutilated woman, he could not help but wonder at his true motivations.

This place shouldn't be here, Rufiere had said.

"Then neither should we," Jakk muttered.

"What?" Barr marched ahead, face glowing with the thrill of recent bloodletting.

"Nothing," Jakk said.

Barr smiled gently. "You always were the weak one, Jakk."

"And you're always the first to remind me of that." Jakk looked at Rufiere and Leeza, and their expressions were unreadable. They followed, that was all. And Barr was the strongest—outwardly, at least—and so it was him they chose to follow. So simple, yet it was a hierarchy that had been maintained for over a year.

Barr glanced up the slope at the small machines still harvesting the purple plant. "You're too easily distracted," he said. "That's all." He bit the woman's sliced-off thumb between his teeth and smiled.

Leeza laughed out loud and Rufiere shook his head, and Jakk somehow found a smile to present to Barr. "You're sick," he said.

"Thank you," Barr muttered. He opened his mouth and caught the dropped thumb, shoving it into his pocket. "I'll string that later. May be more to go with it before the day's out." Then he turned and walked down the hillside. His feet crunched in the loose shale, sending small drifts down towards the lower levels of mist that shrouded the valley.

There's no need, Jakk wanted to say. *These people aren't part of what we were doing.* But he could not find his voice. Silence had always been his greatest weakness.

———

SUNLIGHT FADED, the mists closed in around them like a false night, and the ground they walked on turned from shale to soil. They saw no more people or machines, but there was evidence of both. The hills had once been farmed and here and there were fields still planted with crops. Much of the crop was the same purple plant the machines had been harvesting farther up the slopes, but there was also a tall, light green grass, and a pungent yellow crop that seemed to sway with a life of its own. Leeza stepped into a clump of these yellow plants and they turned to her, leaning in from all sides as though attracted by her life force. She swept her sword around her and cut them away, and Jakk listened hard for their screams.

The mist was heavy and it dampened their clothing. Their weapons quickly beaded with moisture, and they started perspiring in the close heat of the valley. It made a trap for the sun, and once contained below this level of mist there was no escape.

"What are we looking for?" Jakk asked.

"Stuff," Rufiere said. "Spoils of war."

"The war's over," Jakk said.

"Fuck's sake." Leeza mumbled, but her words carried.

"And you think now it's over there's a place for people like us?" Barr asked without breaking step or turning around.

"I'm a blacksmith," Jakk said. It was the first time he had thought about that for a long time, and the memory of his former occupation now seemed like the recollection of someone else. His forge, his tools, his customers, the man sweating as he moulded and cast horseshoes and other metalwork now seemed like a person he could never know. He tried to recall the smell of the fire, but the valley was filled with other scents today.

"You're a killer," Barr said. He carried on walking, as if they were talking about the weather or something equally banal. "Have been for a long time. Remember the first person you killed? I do. Soyaran woman wearing a green dress, long yellow hair. Quite a pretty face beneath the scars."

Jakk remembered. She'd smiled at him and he'd felt wanted, and then she had come at him with fingers hooked into claws.

"She had enough venom beneath her nails to kill you ten times over," Leeza said.

"Knife to the throat," Rufiere said. "Then you severed her spine when she was down so she couldn't crawl."

Yes, Jakk could recall everything. Her smile, her smell, the sway of her hair as she came at him, the feeling of the world moving around him as opposed to him moving through the world, slipping aside, avoiding her hands and green-tinged fingernails as he swept a knife across her throat. The gush of blood that he was keen to avoid. The thump of her hitting the ground, and she was still smiling as she crawled at him. He'd stuck his sword between her shoulder blades and leaned on it, then let her bleed to death before him. She had wanted him dead, that was for certain. He could still remember her face.

"She wanted me dead," Jakk said.

"We're all changed."

"You're a fruit grower, Barr. You had a farm on the Cantrass Plains, and you left your wife and three sons to come down here and fight. Wanted to make enough money to go back and buy more land, a machine to tend your crops, another to dig a water well."

"I'm no longer a farmer," Barr said, stopping and turning around. "And all the machines are dead."

"I just don't see—"

"There could be anything down here!" Barr said. He gestured at the mist and headed off again, and the anger was apparent in the length of his stride.

It turned out that he was right.

THE MIST began to clear, revealing a wide swathe of valley below and ahead of them. And it was more than beautiful. The hillsides were gentler down here and planted heavily with yellow and purple crop, a few wilder areas speckled green and grey. Not far from where they now stood a small waterfall came down from the cliff face, tumbling from protruding rocks, whispering secrets to the air and splashing a small rainbow into existence at its base. A network of streams originated in the hills where they now stood and merged in the distance, forming a wider river that wended its way northward. The valley there was still swathed in sheets of mist, and more coloured rainbow sheens arced from one side to the other.

It was also instantly apparent that the valley did not belong. Rufiere was right; it should not be here. Jakk had never seen anywhere so unknown and alien, and it was not the landscape or what was upon it that gave that impression. It was the sheer size and feel of the place. Here was a valley unaware of the fact that magic was no longer in the land, and where machines still drew power from and communed with that magic. Here was a place where the sky seemed shielded by a constant mist, and yet sunlight shone through and made the plants grow, the waters shine. It gave the feeling of being somewhere else entirely, and when Jakk turned and looked back the way they had come, he could not picture the plains of Noreela lying above that low cloud cover.

"There," Barr said.

"I see vineyards, and plenty of cattle," Leeza said.

Rufiere frowned down into the valley, passing his small tatty book from one hand to the other. *It's him I can work on,* Jakk thought. *He doesn't think we should be here either.*

The idea of turning around and retreating on his own crossed his mind again, but it felt impossible. He was here with the others, and he would do his best to make sure they walked out as easily as they had walked in.

"Good," Barr said. "A meal, wine, and then some village virgins to fuck."

"Speak for yourself," Leeza said.

Barr glanced around at Jakk and Rufiere, smiling an awful smile. "We'll let you watch, dear Leeza."

"Charmed, I'm sure."

Barr started for the village they could see nestled on the valley floor. The river flowed through it, and tall trees grew throughout the settlement, separating large, solid-looking houses and providing areas of alternating light and shade.

From a distance it could have been anywhere, but as they closed in Jakk realised that it was nowhere at all.

An old man approached them. He seemed cautious but harmless. When he saw their weapons he paused, then turned and started running back the way he had come. Leeza took him down with a crossbow bolt to the lower back. She ran to him, and he was still screaming when she knelt on his back, lifted his head by the hair and hacked into his throat.

Jakk paused and closed his eyes, but that smell hit him again. Sweet, heavy and promising wonders. And he suddenly needed to know what it was.

———

THEY SAW more machines as they neared the village. Two sat motionless beside a wide stream, and to begin with Jakk thought they were dead. They were sunk in the mud at the edge of the stream, stone hides green with moss, metal protuberances brown with rust where they extended out and down into the water. Some patches of skin on their backs sprouted thick black hairs, and it was when Jakk saw the wisps of steam issuing from the ends of these hairs that he realised that the machines were not dead at all. Whatever their purpose by the side of that stream, they were as alive as those they had seen on the high hillsides.

They walked on, closing on the village, and Barr led the way. He had a natural arrogance about him that had been there even before they had started fighting in Ventgoria, and it had served him well as he blooded himself, scaring the enemy and unsettling his comrades. He projected a sense of immortality, or not caring about death. Both were effective.

There were heavy stone bridges crossing the streams, and when they came to the river they followed its course towards the village. There was a well-worn trail here, lined with stone slabs to prevent it becoming too marshy for travel, its route carved through small rises and mounds of heavy rock. Jakk recognised the signs from a hundred other places in Noreela, and he knew that machines had made this road.

From somewhere came a deep, pounding roar that filled the air with its bass tones and thumped at the ground, reverberating up through their feet and into the bones of their legs. Jakk's stomach rolled and he gagged, swallowing hard to hold down the vomit.

"Alarm," Barr said. "They know we're not good news." He sounded delighted.

Jakk scanned the village for signs of opposition but saw none. Machines, yes. One of them sat beside the road where it passed the first village building, gathering something from the ground with long, swooping passes of its fluid limbs. It seemed to pay them no heed. Another drifted from one building to the next, slamming shutters. He saw the glint of a metal machine cast into the wall of a house beside the river, and fleshy appendages pulsed as water flowed through them into the structure. But none of them seemed ready to fight.

It confused him. If the villagers were wary enough to have constructed some sort of alarm, surely they would have weapons of their own?

"We shouldn't be too confident," he said.

Barr scoffed. "Pah! I smell weakness on the air as strong as shit on a shepherd's foot."

Leeza laughed. "I smell no shit, but I *do* smell food." Her arm was still bleeding from the cut she'd put there after killing the old man, and she smeared the blood on her thumb, put it to her mouth. She raised an eyebrow at Jakk. "I'm hungry for something rare."

Jakk suddenly caught that scent again, the rich smell that had been wafting at them ever since they had entered the valley. He closed his eyes briefly and breathed deep, and when he looked again he saw where the smell originated. Along the muddy river bank to their right grew a profusion of red flowers. They were beautiful, yet something about them unsettled. He had never seen blooms like this before; the way they hung heavy on impossibly thin stems, the unnatural brightness of their colour. And the aroma was more animal than plant, the meaty scent of something living opened up to the air and venting blood. *Blood roses*, Jakk thought. As if to acknowledge that name he saw the effect on the mud beneath them, wet and glistening but not with river water. The colour was difficult to discern against the dark mud, but he had seen the stickiness of spilled blood many times before.

As he watched, one rose seemed to bow down towards the ground, stem bending almost double. A pearl of blood dropped from it—shockingly red—and then the rose sprang up again, as if relieved of a great weight.

"Like the land's bleeding," Leeza said. For once, the bravado had slipped from her voice.

"This place shouldn't be here," Rufiere said.

Barr did not stop walking, but he said nothing. Jakk noted that he stayed in the lead so none of them could see his face.

———

"YOU TOLD me you fought in the War!" Bindy says.

"And I did!" Jakk says. "Just not against the Krotes." He is moving quickly around their small home, hurrying to gather what they will need while trying not to startle Romana. She did not see him kill Barr, and for that he is grateful. But soon they will have to go outside.

"I don't understand," Bindy says.

Jakk gathers up a handful of water skins and slings them over his shoulder. They will need filling. They have one horse, an old nag, but she will have to do, she can carry Romana and some of what they need, and when they're far enough away he will send them—

"Jakk!" Bindy almost shouts, and he does not like the edge of panic in her voice. "Jakk, I just saw what happened. You owe me an explanation, don't you think?"

He turns to his wife and moves so that he is between her and Romana. Clasping Bindy's shoulders he leans in close, touching foreheads, smelling the fear on her breath. He hopes it is not fear of him. "We're in danger," he whispers. "For now that's all you need to know. We can't just wait. We need to leave here, and I'll tell you everything as we go."

"Leave?"

"Go far away."

"This is our home."

Jakk shakes his head. "Not anymore. Maybe later we can come back again...." He steps back and shakes his head, panic threatening to undo him.

"Daddy?" Romana says quietly, and her plea does not help him.

"Roma, I need you to go to your room and get some clothes," Jakk says. "Not too much, because the old horse has to carry everything."

"Where are we going?" she asks, eyes wide. She has never left the forest before.

"For a walk," Jakk says. "An adventure! Like the stories I tell you at night about the Voyagers."

"We're going on a Voyage?" she asks, anxiety changing instantly to excitement.

"Yes," he says. "We're going exploring."

"What will we find?"

I'm not sure, he thinks. *Maybe nothing. Maybe we'll never even get away from the forest.* "Somewhere else," he says.

As if content with Jakk's obscure answer Romana rushes into her room, and he hears her rummaging around in there, gathering things for their voyage of discovery.

"We're running?" Bindy asks.

"Yes," he says quietly.

"From what happened to him?" She nods at the closed door as though Barr is standing there.

Jakk nods. Neither of them wants to mention that it was he who had finally killed Barr. *He was dying anyway,* he thinks, but it's only something to say to Bindy. He realises that he feels no remorse at all. That is hardly a surprise.

Bindy stares at him for a beat, and her strength is apparent in her stance. He really doesn't think he could have lived with a weak person for so long. She lifts him up when he's low, guides him through dark times, and when he has nightmares she is always there for him when he sweats himself awake. She has never asked about those nightmares. He knows that she assumes they're leftovers from the Cataclysmic War, and now that she has heard his own conflict was apart from that great battle there's confusion in her eyes.

"Tell me I don't have to be scared of you, Jakk."

His heart almost breaks. "Bindy...."

She sighs and closes her eyes. When she looks at him again she smiles. "But as soon as we're away, you need to talk," she says.

Jakk nods because he finds he cannot speak. Tears threaten, and out of everything that should inspire them—fear of what had come, the pain of past times dredged up again, the blood roses he had smelled upon returning from his hunt—it's shame that brings them on. He has lied to Bindy for so long, and now he feels like a traitor.

"Everything," he says. "You'll hear it all."

THEY ARE ready to leave by mid-afternoon. Bindy keeps their daughter in the house packing their saddle bags while Jakk drags Barr's body between the trees. He does not attempt to bury him, nor to chant his wraith down, because this mercenary deserves neither. Jakk hopes that his spirit finds only torture in death, a fitting punishment for everything Barr had done in life, and as he walks back into the clearing he feels a presence behind him, desperate and lost. That almost makes him smile.

As they leave Bindy is sobbing quietly. Jakk chats to Romana to cover the sound of her mother's tears. His daughter looks at him with a frown on her innocent little face, and he knows that she's wondering about the weapons he carries. She has seen him bearing the bow and quiver a thousand times before when he goes hunting, but everything else is strange to her. The sword on his belt, the knives, the throwing stars fixed to the straps across his chest, the slideshock on his arm, the crossbow hanging from the old horse's saddle…she has never seen them before. And in truth, Jakk has not taken good care of them at all. The stars are dulled, the sword speckled with rust, and he is worried that the carefully balanced slideshock mechanism has seized completely. But his first priority is to leave. If Barr knew how to find him, then it will as well. That machine. That thing.

He's surprised only that it has taken so long.

THEY WALK all afternoon and into the evening, and by the time dusk falls they are at the western boundary of Pengulfin Woods, staring out at the beginnings of the Cantrass Plains. Jakk decides to camp one more night in the shelter of trees, because that is a place the three of them know. He wishes he had questioned Barr some more, but anything the dying man said could have been lies. *All* of it could have been lies. But there were the blood roses blooming across his stomach, and there was no way could he have lied about those. Jakk had only ever seen them down in that folded valley, smelled them there, and now that they bloomed again and processed Noreelan air....

There was no escape. He was fooling himself. He had known that from the moment he saw Barr, dying on the ground outside his home. But what else could he do but run?

The machines were dead. They littered the landscape like ruined buildings of the Noreelans' ancestors, rotting, crumbling, rusting, fading away into the land's bloody history even while the present bled into the damned future. Perhaps his only hope lay in the possibility that whatever had come for them would yield to the same fate.

BY THE time they entered the village it seemed like a ghost town. They had seen some movement on their way along the road, but now it looked abandoned, as if every inhabitant had fled or vanished. But it was obvious from what was left behind that the villagers were all hiding.

Several chimneys still gushed smoke. A door swayed open and closed in the slight breeze, and one building a hundred steps into the village was fronted by a makeshift table, spices and other wares laid out for prospective buyers to view. A wolf lay underneath, still tied to one table leg by a length of rope. It raised its head as they approached, growled softly and then went back to sleep.

"Something strange here," Leeza said.

"You mean besides everyone hiding from us?" Rufiere asked.

Barr tried to laugh, but it came out like a gasp. "Our reputation precedes us," he said.

Jakk shook his head. "Leeza's right. Why should they fear us? We're all tooled up, true, but lots of people carry weapons nowadays."

"That woman," Rufiere said. "That old man Leeza killed."

"I killed him because he ran," she said.

"I don't care," Rufiere continued. "Didn't you all notice how surprised they were to see us?"

"They're not used to visitors," Jakk said. It was obvious. The village had the feel of a place never visited and rarely left. There were no posts for tying horses, and no sign that there were any stables or grazing fields nearby. The few shops they could see displayed fruit and vegetables, leather goods and metal wares that could all have been manufactured locally. And there were no signs. What village or town ran itself without having to point the way? If there was a tavern it went unadvertised, the shops were obvious only from their window displays, and several other buildings had blank façades which could have hidden anything inside.

"You said this valley shouldn't be here," Jakk said to Rufiere. "I believed you from the start."

"Well it is here, and we're here, and I'm not leaving until I find something worth taking with me." Barr walked on ahead, still not turning around to look at them.

He's scared, Jakk thought. *He's actually scared, and for him that'll be a first. He lost it a year ago, during that massacre in the Terrenian marshes, and since then he's been a blank. But now....*

"I'm scared," Rufiere said.

"Then leave," Barr said from ahead. "A three-way share suits me better."

There was a loud crash from somewhere across the village, the source of the sound hidden from view by the buildings and huge trees.

The four mercenaries moved apart and drew their weapons, instincts honed in years of fighting together taking over. Barr and Leeza hurried for the shelter of a low house to their left. Jakk and Rufiere went right, passing beneath a stone arch to a tumbled-down wall.

The crashing noise came again, followed by a metallic snap, and then both sounds yet again. The regularity could have been footsteps.

"That sounds like a *big* machine," Rufiere said.

Jakk sheathed his sword and strung an arrow in his bow. He could see along the street from here, and if someone or something emerged from between buildings he'd have time to shoot them before they reached him.

"Maybe they're trying to scare us away?" Jakk asked. He looked at Rufiere but the tall soldier was concentrating hard on the sounds.

"It's not coming closer," he said at last. After three more repeats, the noises stopped.

Barr and Leeza broke cover and dashed along the street. There were thirty places where an enemy may be hiding, and it was nowhere near safe. But Barr thought he was indestructible.

Jakk ran back through the stone arch and along the opposite side of the road, and he heard Rufiere behind him.

No windows burst open to unleash a hail of arrows. No trip-wire sprang from the dust to slice into their shins. There was no rushing attack from the shadows between buildings or beneath trees, and no sense that any attack was about to come. The inhabitants of this place were well and truly hidden away.

Perhaps when they reached the centre of the village the trap would spring.

Jakk glanced up at one of the huge trees as they ran through its shadow. It was adorned with brightly-coloured streamers, each of them ending just above head height, and there were climbing slats fixed into its wide trunk. He paused and scanned the branches for shadows that should not be there, but the tree appeared empty.

Barr whistled from along the street and waved Jakk and Rufiere on. He pointed to his eyes, then nodded around the corner of the building he leaned against. *Found something.*

When Jakk reached Barr and Leeza, they were breathing heavily from their dash.

"Something there," Barr said. "Look. The building behind that old man. Something there, and that's what we heard, the whole place being locked up."

Jakk knelt down and peered around Barr's legs, keeping his bow at the ready.

They were at the centre of the village, and it was marked by a large circular area occupied by only one building. The structure was no higher than the tallest man, and consisted of an inverted bowl shape with openings spaced at regular intervals around its sloping wall. These openings—windows or doors—were covered with heavy timber shutters, and across each shutter were locked two thick iron bars. An old man stood before the building, watching the mercenaries with a blank expression. He bore no weapons, and his simple clothing hung on his gaunt frame. Jakk thought he was the oldest man he had ever seen.

The area all around the building was spotted with clumps of the blood roses. The ground beneath each bloom was dark and damp.

"Could be a trap," Rufiere said.

"No," Barr said. "There's something in there they don't want us to see, and that only makes me want to see it more." He stepped fully from behind the building and started walking.

The old man suddenly looked terrified. There was something about duty and responsibility in his stance, but as his nervous gaze switched from Barr, to Jakk, to Leeza and Rufiere, it was obvious that he was a reluctant guardian.

Barr paused six steps from the old man and wielded his sword.

Jakk and the other formed a semi-circle behind Barr, blocking the man's escape. Jakk offered a small smile and tried to exude calmness, but the villager was shaking now, and he looked at Barr as the obvious leader of their group.

"What's in there?" Barr asked, nodding at the building.

The old man frowned, and for a beat Jakk thought he did not understand their language. *This place shouldn't be here*, Rufiere had said, and Jakk felt a chill. If this man did not speak Noreelan then they were truly somewhere they should have never found.

And then the man spoke. "Who...who are you?"

"Ask me another question and I'll kill you," Barr said. He lifted his grisly necklace and used the dead woman's still-tacky finger to point at the man. "You want a place on here?"

The man's eyes went wide and he shook his head.

"So, what's in there?"

"I can't say. I can't tell you. It's...forbidden. For anyone like you. Anyone from beyond the folded valley."

"Folded valley," Rufiere echoed. He was still holding his short spear, but in his other hand the supposed Book of Ways hung open, his thumb stroking the page.

The old man turned to Rufiere. "*You* understand."

Barr stepped forward and spiked the man's shoulder with his sword. His rough shirt parted and darkened with blood, and the old man cried out.

The village seemed to gasp. *We're being watched*, Jakk thought. Rufiere glanced at him and frowned, obviously sensing the same.

"Don't piss with us, old man," Leeza said, perhaps trying to save him from Barr's full fury. She stepped forward and shoved him to the ground, standing on his wounded shoulder. "Folded valleys can stay folded, far as I care, but there's something in there—"

"It *should* have stayed folded," the man said. He was grimacing in pain, but his confusion seemed more intense.

"If you have a key for those locks, best take it out and hand it to me right now."

The village sighed this time, a gentle, long exhalation. Jakk looked around and saw columns of steam rising from a dozen places around them, issuing from tall metal tubes that protruded above rooftops. He had seen features like this before, and they always belonged to machines.

"You have machines living in the valley," Jakk said.

"Of course," the man said. Leeza took her foot from his shoulder and let him sit up.

"Why? How? Machines are dead."

The man shook his head sadly, looking down at the ground between his legs. He looked wretched.

Jakk kicked at a blood rose growing close by, setting it swaying on its thin but strong stem. He watched the man, whose head rose slightly to see what he was doing. The man now looked angry.

"What are these?" Jakk asked.

"I can't tell you," the man said, but his expression said, *I won't tell you.*

Barr shouted an unintelligible roar of rage and kicked out at the man's head. The crunching sound was sickening and final, and the man collapsed to the ground, twitching. His eyes rolled up in his head and he started foaming at the mouth.

Jakk looked away from the dying man and crushed one of the blooms down beneath his boot, pressing slowly. It burst onto the ground and spurted bright red sap across the dust.

The village growled. The sound came from all around them, a low, meaty rumble that threatened the air they breathed.

The tall metal columns gushed steam again, the outpourings more intense this time, pressure higher.

"What's that?" Rufiere said. His voice shook.

Jakk looked up from the crushed flower and across at Barr, and he realised then that the difference between them was simply a matter of control. They had both killed many people, and the faces of those he had killed—in a fight, and in cold blood—had started to haunt Jakk's dreams. But he knew when to stop, and that time had come and gone. Barr knew as well, but he could not find any way to stop. Perhaps it was madness, and maybe that in itself was a defence, but he would keep fighting and killing until he was killed himself.

Barr approached the building. "Doesn't matter what that is," he said. "What matters is here."

"I think we should leave," Jakk said. "Barr, I don't think there's anything here for us. It's a folded valley."

"And what the fuck is a folded valley?" Leeza asked.

Jakk lifted his arms and gestured around them. "I really don't think we want to find out."

Leeza's knuckles tightened on her sword. They had fought long and hard together, and this was the first time Jakk had felt threatened by one of his own.

He shook his head.

Barr struck at the iron bars locked across a wooden shutter. Sparks flew, but nothing seemed to shift. The locks were strong.

"Rufiere, your spear."

Rufiere lobbed the spear to Barr, who caught it from the air and wedged it beneath one of the bars. He pulled slowly, judging the strain, and then with one heave tugged the bar's hinged end from the shutter's frame.

Jakk turned his back on the others and looked around, his bow at the ready, quiver full, every weapon he bore familiar to him, each blade and throwing star responsible for at least one of those dead faces that haunted him. He tried not to see the spread of blood roses, because now they made the village square look like a battlefield.

Another breaking sound from behind him, and then he heard one of the shutters lifted open and dropped back against the building's sloping wall.

"What in the Black is that?" Leeza said. Her voice was quiet and hoarse.

Barr's breathing came fast, and whatever he tried to say came out as a croak.

Jakk turned to see what they had found, and he only caught a glimpse of something red and wet inside the domed building before a roar of rage rose up behind him.

The villagers had emerged. There were scores of them, maybe hundreds, spewing from doorways, pouring out from the shadows between buildings, some of them slipping down the abundant coloured streamers in the trees. None carried true weapons, but there were sticks and tools, rocks and knives, and they glared at the mercenaries with fury in their eyes.

They were no longer afraid.

———

HE DREAMS that the thing in the pit has tracked them through the woods, and that it takes Bindy and Romana down from the horse, slaughters the animal and hangs his wife and daughter from a low tree like living ribbons. It teases him. Jakk is watching from a distance and he is either hidden, or trapped and unable to move; it's difficult to tell in the dream. It touches them with some of it its long appendages, and where it touches blood roses grow. The stems stretch the skin first, forcing it from below and then splitting it, emerging in blood like a grotesque parody of human birth. They do not scream, but they are awake, both of them watching in fascination as their bodies host these mysterious blooms. He smells the blood roses then, and the scent impacts hard because it is the only thing he can smell in the dream. Even though he looks around and sees pine trees leaking sap, violetbells speckling the ground between trees and honey cones hanging all around, all he can smell are these flowers that should not be here. *Never should have been in the folded valley, either,* he says. *Rufiere was right, it should not have been there, we should have found* nothing.

The thing looks at him then, even though he's not sure it actually has any eyes. And mouthless, it smiles.

HE RISES from sleep and nightmare certain that he is being watched. He lies for a moment with his eyes open, trying not to move, and then he remembers that Bindy and Romana are sleeping behind him.

Jakk sits up quickly and turns to where his family should be. And they are still there, covered with thick blankets, Romana huddled in to Bindy's side for warmth. His wife mutters something in her sleep and shifts slightly, turning her face away from the dawn.

Their old horse is standing apart from them, tied loosely to a tree. He can see its ribs moving as it breathes, and its head shakes slightly, tail swishes.

Just a dream, he thinks, but he reaches over and pulls the blankets from his wife and daughter anyway. There are no blood roses blooming on their skin. That confuses him, and he frowns and shakes his head, trying to shake the remnants of his dream away. Perhaps it was still loose in there, planting ideas that should have faded with sleep.

"No blood roses," he whispers. His wife opens her eyes and stares around in panic. She looks at him and does not know him, but a beat later recognition arrives.

"I've had such dreams," she says.

Jakk nods. "Sleeping under the stars. They touch your mind without a roof over your head to keep them out."

She pulls her arm gently from beneath Romana's head and glances up and down her daughter's body, as if searching for blooms as well. "I dreamed of those flowers."

Jakk draws in a startled breath and that's when he realises what is wrong. He has risen from his dream and cast those roses aside, but he can smell them still.

"Bindy...." he says, but she is already standing, seeing the warning in his eyes.

"Romana?"

"Leave her asleep for now." Jakk stands quickly and reaches for his weapons. *No time to tie on the slideshock*, he thinks. *Crossbow is old and hasn't been oiled for years.* He tugs the sword from its sheath leaning against the saddle, and plucks the bow from where he had stuck it in the ground.

"What is it?" Bindy asks.

"Whatever killed Barr is here." Yet again the realities of Barr's death hang between them, but Bindy remains silent.

Jakk watches the spaces between the trees.

"But what *is* it?"

"I'm not sure," he says. "He called it 'it', and he called it 'them'." He sees her looking at him from the corner of his eye but he does not turn. He needs to be alert, and if Bindy starts him talking now....

There is movement in the forest. A shape passes from one tree to the next, a fleeting shadow that could have been cast by something crossing the sun. Jakk holds his breath and strings an arrow, pulling back to give it some tension. He can swing around and fire within a heartbeat if he needs to. He watches for more movement, and when he thinks of that machine they saw in the pit he knows that he will see it, hear it and smell it long before it is upon them.

But still it killed Leeza and Rufiere.

He steps closer to Bindy where she stands above Romana. He can hear her short, light breaths.

Something else moves, a pale shape between trees. Jakk brings the bow up, pulling on the string as he does so, and fires the arrow. It whistles away into the forest and disappears without hitting anything. Even before he loses sight of it he has another arrow strung.

"I'm scared," Bindy says. "Can't we just go? Can't we run."

"Mummy?" Romana says. As the girl wakes she sees her parents standing above her, Jakk bearing the bow and a stern expression, and she immediately begins to cry.

They emerge from between the trees. While Jakk is looking down at his frightened daughter, and Bindy is kneeling to give comfort, and for a beat his attention is distracted, that is when they choose to come.

Jakk senses the movement and looks up, but it is too late. They are already close, and amazement freezes him long enough for the lead woman to knock the bow aside and lash out. Her fist is cool and hard and it strikes his temple, dazing him and driving him down.

He falls onto his back and looks up at the things come to kill him.

Bindy shouts, Romana sees them and screams, and Jakk tries to rise to protect his family.

The woman who struck him hisses. The two thin metal pipes protruding from each shoulder spurt steam, and a sound comes from her mouth that is unmistakeably a warning. Her eyes are pure silver and reflect the strengthening dawn light with a metallic sheen.

Jakk glances across at his slideshock.

"I'll kill you before your muscles obey your brain's order

to move," a low voice says. The woman squats beside him and those pipes emit another puff of steam.

Bindy is holding Romana, pressing the girl's face against her chest so that she does not have to see, and looking intently at Jakk so that *she* cannot see. But there are four of them, and they are incredible, and to not look is impossible.

There are two men and two women. They all have steam pipes, though the other woman has three from each shoulder. They all possess those metallic eyes as well, and grilles in the sides of their necks beneath which red stuff seems to pulse, and their fingernails are a similar silver as though their hands are metal but for the skin. The junction between metal and flesh—at their necks, and the quick of their nails—is red and inflamed, glistening here and there with pus.

"What are you?" Jakk asks.

The woman fists her hands and metal scrapes metal. "Children of the heart and mind," she says.

"Folded people." The name comes to Jakk from nowhere but seems to make sense.

"Maybe." She smiles, and her teeth are grey as damp stone.

"Please," he says, but she does not let him finish. *Please don't hurt my family*, he wants to say. *Please let them go.*

"Please is just what the others said too."

"What others?" But he knows.

"The others who came with you. The ones who destroyed our home and killed our people."

"I never wanted to—"

"And yet you did." The woman stands and walks to Bindy and Romana, and her movement is awkward and accompanied by grating, grinding sound. Pinkish fluid drips from the pipes on her back.

"Don't hurt my family," he manages to say, and the woman and her three companions look at him. Unlike the thing in his dreams they do have mouths, and their smiles are obvious. But there is no humour there. Only hatred.

"Whether they're hurt or not is entirely up to you," the woman says. She nods to one of the men and he kneels beside Jakk's wife and child.

"No!" Bindy screams. She lashes out with one hand, the other still holding Romana's face against her chest. The man catches her hand and squeezes. Beneath Bindy's shriek of agony, Jakk hears bones crunch and snap.

"Leave them!" he shouts, trying to stand. The woman is beside him again in a beat, planting a hand on his chest and pushing him back down, pressing him into the ground. He can hardly breathe. He feels an old cracked rib beginning to go again, but he can understand nothing other than the threat to his family.

Bindy curls around Romana, her face pale with pain. She's sweating. Her hand is bleeding. When the man pulls Romana from her grasp, there is nothing she can do.

"*Please!*" Jakk shouts again, and the woman smiles down at him with grave-slab teeth, eyes glinting yellow as dawn flames through the forest.

"Yes," she says, "that's *exactly* what they said."

Jakk struggles, but to no avail. For the first time in his life he is utterly helpless. He has to watch as Romana is dragged away from Bindy, his wife crying and reaching for their child with her unbroken hand. He has to hear his daughter's scream. And then the woman holding him down moves aside so that he has a clear view, as the other three folded people—machines, humans or bastard offspring of the two—pierce their forearms with metallic fingernails and dribble blood across Romana's bared stomach.

Jakk bites his lip and draws his own blood, but he does not wake from the nightmare.

The roses quickly begin to sprout.

———

PERHAPS IT was the old man they had killed, but Jakk thought not. It was more likely the shutter Barr had forced open that enraged the villagers so much.

They closed in on the building and then paused, keeping the same distance all around. Their eyes flickered down to the open hatch, at the invaders standing before it and back again. There was accusation there, and anger, and Jakk saw the promise of violence. He knew it well enough.

"You should not have come here," a short, old woman said.

"We were walking, we found a valley and we entered," Barr said. "We're entitled."

" 'Entitled'?" the old woman said, eyebrows raising. She looked Barr up and down as though viewing a new sheebok at market. "You're part of the sickness in the land, and you say you're entitled to bring it to us?"

"I bring nothing," Barr said. Jakk could already hear his patience withering, and looking sidelong at his comrade he could sense the violence about to erupt. "But I'm more than willing to take," Barr continued, backing at the opening in the side of the building.

"No!" the woman said. "You mustn't. You can't!"

" 'Can't'?" Barr said, mimicking her voice.

"We weren't part of the Cataclysmic War," Jakk said, stepping forward. If he could halt the flow of this tide, stem the wave of violence that tainted the air, perhaps they could leave in peace. Maybe he could talk to Barr. "We're going north, that's all, and when we came across your valley—"

"They killed Raddock, as well," someone said. "I found him on the edge of the village, by the stream. His head's almost off."

"And Mayria has not returned from seeding," another voice added, breaking with fear.

The old woman closed her eyes. "More power for the heart and mind," she whispered solemnly. It was a prayer Jakk had never heard before, but Noreela was full of such sects.

"It's you that shouldn't be here," Rufiere said. He stepped forward and held out his book as if to show them all.

"Rufiere!" Barr said, but the tall soldier ignored him.

"This valley shouldn't be here, it's not shown, it's not *right*."

"More right than what's left of Noreela," the woman said. Old she may have been, but her voice was young and full of fury. "It's a land slaughtered by greed, and you come down here, kill my friend and tell me it's us who shouldn't be here?"

"But you're not on the map!" Rufiere said, as if this would settle everything.

"Maps!" the woman spat.

"Rufiere, back in line," Barr said softly.

"What is this place?" Jakk said. He could see the villagers' eyes when they looked at Rufiere, as if he had exposed a great secret. "What are those blood roses we saw?"

"They're good for us," the old woman said. She chewed on her lip for a moment as if mulling something over. The villagers shifted, nervous and unsettled. There must have been a hundred of them facing the four mercenaries, the threat still evident.

"We don't want to kill you all," Barr said. "Well, in all honestly, these three don't want to kill you all. Me...I'd happily put you to the sword. More trophies for me, eh?" He held up his thumb necklace and chuckled.

Jakk saw the old woman's eyes widen slightly as she saw what Barr wore. Perhaps she noticed the fresh blood there.

"All this talk of killing," she said. "You can't leave."

"What?" Jakk said.

"You can't. If you leave you'll bring Noreela back to us."

"You think you can stop us?" Barr said.

The woman closed her eyes and dipped her head, and as she spoke the other villagers squatted and touched the ground at their feet. "Heart and mind, keep us well. Heart and mind, keep us wise. Heart and mind, protect us." She opened her eyes again, and when she looked at the mercenaries her face reflected murder. "Heart and mind...give us strength."

"No," Jakk whispered. Rufiere and Leeza backed away slightly, but Barr stepped forward, eager. The first stone struck him in the chest.

THE SHOOTS are both beautiful and gruesome, redolent of new life and harbingers of death. Romana stops screaming as they spread questing tendrils across the surface of her skin, flesh quivering beneath their prickle, and she looks from their rapid growth to her father's eyes, begging him for help. She is beyond crying now. Shock has her in its grasp and the strange woman holding her down eases back, realising that her work is done.

There are no blooms yet, but the blood rose flowers are still unmistakable within their closed bulbs. Even now Jakk can see the colour. They're like blood boils waiting to burst, and he knows that when they do their smell will add to the scent of the four people who have come for him. Or four machines. The distinction no longer seems to matter.

Two of the folded people move quickly to the unconscious Bindy, their blood dripping across her neck and exposed legs.

"No," Jakk whispers, but when he tries to move the woman presses down even harder, crushing the air from his lungs. "What...what do you want?" he says.

The blood splashes sprout scarlet shoots on Bindy's body. Where the blood touched her crushed hand and broken skin they are already a hand's-width tall, and they seem ready to bloom.

"You want your family to live?" the woman says. Jakk is staring at her face upside down, and from that angle the pipes seem like horns. They steam, she smiles.

"Of course," Jakk says.

"They're important to you?"

"Yes."

She laughs, a bitter snort. She is silent for a while. "I had family," she says. "You killed them."

Jakk cannot find anything to say. An apology would feel so trite, an explanation pointless. There was nothing that could be explained, and "sorry" held no power.

"It made us," the woman says. "Put us together from what was left and sent us out of the valley. It took a long time. You almost killed the heart and mind, and you left the valley weak. Unable to help itself."

"I wanted to leave," Jakk says. "It was Barr...he was the one...."

"Your actions made me, not your intentions."

Jakk finds that the woman holds his attention now, not his suffering wife and child, and perhaps there is some small escape there for a while.

"We're such a long way from the valley," the woman says. "You have to take us back."

"Back?"

The woman nods. Her silvery eyes are expressionless. He hears a rattling sound as she speaks, as though something is broken inside. She could be laughing or crying, Jakk cannot tell. "We've had our revenge. It made us for retribution, but we've lost our way. We come and go, but we cannot find the valley. It's folded to us, hidden away, and...."

"You think I know where it is?"

"You have to know." The woman lifts her hand from his chest, and with her other hand she turns his face back to his family. The roses bloom, dripping their thick red sap, and the other three folded people breathe deeply of the scent.

"We can't keep doing this," the woman says. "The strength is good, but the killing is not."

"My family...."

"They can be saved. It's slow, they have time. Show us the valley and we'll release them."

"No," Jakk says. "No, I don't know where it is, I don't understand."

"Your friends denied us as well," the woman says. "The woman died fighting. And right until the end, Rufiere claimed that we shouldn't exist."

"What happened to him?"

"We seeded him as we've seeded your wife and child. Sat with him. The blooms give us our strength, as the heart and mind draws strength from the valley blooms."

"Barr told me Rufiere was dead."

"He is. It took three moons."

Jakk shakes his head but he cannot deny what is happening. "Free them," he says, trying to keep the plea from his voice. If he sounds strong, perhaps they will find pity.

"Find us the valley and I'll come back and free them myself," the woman says.

I don't know where it is, Jakk thinks. "Of course," he says.

The woman backs away and allows him to stand.

Bindy is still unconscious but her sleep seems deeper now, more certain. And when Jakk walks the few steps to Romana—and the folded people allow him that walk—he can see that her movements are now involuntary. Her eyelids flutter and limbs twitch, but she is somewhere away from here.

"How can we take them if they're not awake?" he asks, struggling to hold the tears. He wants to fight, but he knows that these things can kill him easily. He wants to rage, but he swore long ago never to let that fury take him again. If anything, he feels resigned to what is happening. Guilt is already leaving its stale taste in his mouth.

"They stay here," the woman says. "The faster we move, the sooner you can return."

They'll die, Jakk thinks. *The forest is not a safe place, especially at night.* But saying it will do no good. His uncertain life has passed, and reality has caught up with him at last.

———

THEY CAME like a flood, throwing stones and sticks, mugs and bottles, closing in on them from all sides. Though he had been expecting it, Jakk was still shocked at the sudden violence. Today had started well—their journey north continuing, a place he could call home drawing ever closer—but it would end as many days had ended over the years. Perhaps worse.

Jakk used arrows to begin with, taking down three, and when they drew closer he shouldered the bow and started flinging throwing stars with both hands. They whistled through the air, and every one found flesh. The stars would not kill unless they struck the throat or severed arteries, but a dozen people fell in agony, clutching wounds that held on fast to the barbed weapons.

He wanted to shout at them to stop. Not through fear, although every fight exposed his own mortality, but through hopelessness. There was no reason for this; they were not enemies, and now this village's ground would be tainted with needless blood.

He glanced around at the others and saw that they were enjoying this. They fought with sword and spear, crossbow and slingshot, their killing moves honed over dozens of battles and years of war. Even Rufiere was in the thick of it, perhaps relishing the distraction from wondering where and when they were.

Jakk threw his last metal star and held his left arm out to the side, raising his hand and bracing his legs. When the first villager came close enough—a young man, barely old enough to trim his facial hair—Jakk launched the slingshot. Its weight sprang out, fine wire stretching taut, and a head span through the air.

Nobody seemed to notice. They screamed and screeched, and none of these people were fighters. The were bakers and farmers, shopkeepers and fruit growers, but the sight of a decapitated body spewing blood did nothing to slow them down. Whatever travesty Jakk and the others had performed had driven these people close to madness.

"The dome!" Leeza shouted.

Jakk drew his sword and backed up. The attackers kept on coming. Whatever rage possessed them threw them forward onto the mercenaries' blades, and screams of rage turned to pain. He thrust, withdrew, slashed, stepped back, and he was splashed with their blood.

He half-turned and grabbed hold of a closed shutter, kicking out as he hauled on it. A crossbow bolt whisked by his face and struck a villager in the chest, driving the man back. He dropped a long butcher's knife as he fell.

"Up!" Rufiere shouted.

Jakk slashed out with the sword one more time and then turned, grabbed the shutter properly and hauled himself up onto the stone dome.

The four of them stood there and fended off the attack. Standing atop the structure seemed to make the villagers even more furious, and some of them threw their children up onto the dome. The youngsters' faces reflected the adults' rage, and Jakk kicked out at them, trying to shove them back.

But soon there were too many and he could no longer merely push.

"WHAT IS it?" Jakk shouted. "What have we done?"

The sun had moved across the sky and now touched the western hills. Dead and injured villagers were piled around the base of the building, and others still climbed over them to reach the mercenaries. They were relentless, and so unprepared for a fight that Jakk felt sick at the slaughter. Barr was enjoying it—he was caked in drying blood, white teeth bared in a gruesome grin—and Leeza and Rufiere did what they had to do.

Jakk had stabbed a young boy through the stomach, and he could still see him squirming atop the pile of bodies.

An old woman had come at him with hands clawed, and he had kicked her back several times. But still she came. Soon he would have to kill her.

"What are we doing?" he shouted. In Ventgoria the enemy had been well-defined: Soyaran raiders, emerging from the Poison Forests to take advantage of the war and attack the Ventgorians. And they had been fighters, willing to take on Jakk and the others in their attempts to reach the Ventgorian marshes.

But this was slaughter, pure and simple. And Jakk did not think he could fight on.

A thrown knife struck his arm and sliced to the bone, and he grunted in pain. He lifted his crossbow and shot the thrower in the face.

Barr laughed, and Jakk turned to see the madman watching him.

"What's in there?" Jakk shouted, pointing down at the stone beneath his feet. "What did you see?"

"Why do you think I'm fighting like this?" Barr called. "I want to find out!"

A beat later a great roar sounded. The attackers stopped where they were, seemingly frozen in place, every one of them looking at one of the scores of steam-clouds rising from the tall metal tubes. The tubes vented again, sending that loud roar reverberating around the village. As it died away Jakk heard its echoes from the distant valley slopes, and he wondered whether it could be heard throughout the folded valley.

Barr stepped forward and stabbed a prone man through the back of the neck. He slumped down and started bleeding to death, and the others around him simply moved back.

"Now!" Barr shouted. "While they're like this, kill as many as—"

"Leave them alone, Barr," Jakk said. The others looked at him but he stared them down, teeth grinding together. "No more killing."

"No more?" Barr said. His left hand stole to his belt, reaching for a throwing star. "You shitting coward!"

"You're madder with every day that passes," Jakk said, but at that moment the villagers suddenly moved back. Jakk could hear the cries and groans now, the whimpers of the dying and the sighs of those already dead being walked upon. They left their fallen and pulled back, some limping, a few collapsing and dying as they went. And as if distance from the fight brought reality closer they began to cry, wail and clasp at their faces in disbelief at what was happening.

"The heart!" the old woman who had spoken before shouted.

"The mind!" a man cried.

"Away, away! It's open, stay away!"

Jakk was sweating and shaking, and blood cooled on his skin. Some of it was his own. Fighting the Soyaran, they had always been cautious not to allow their enemies' blood into their own wounds. A lot of their comrades had died that way, poisoned by the poisoners. Here that did not seem to matter, and he felt a momentary, inexplicable elation at emerging from the slaughter relatively unscathed. His arm hurt and gaped when he flexed it, but the pain reminded him he was alive.

The villagers turned and ran. In a few beats they had all vanished again, disappearing into buildings, scampering away between structures, climbing into trees, and all the while they cried.

Barr shouted after them, a war-cry he had favoured in Ventgoria. Jakk was pleased that neither Rufiere nor Leeza took it up.

"So let's see!" Barr said.

"It's holy to them," Jakk said, but he knew no one would listen. And after this, he had to see as well.

What could be worth so much?

———

THEY HAD to pull several bodies aside to see inside the building. It was as if they had died there to block the view.

The sun was setting, but there was still enough light to see what the villagers had been trying to protect.

"Just a big machine," Leeza said, the disappointment evident in her voice. But then they all saw, and Leeza gasped, and none of them really needed to correct her.

At the centre of the space sat a machine, though one that resembled nothing Jakk had ever seen before. Its bulk was organic, a red fleshy body the size of a man from which a score of metallic pipes protruded. They were as long as his forearm, and from most of them came wisps of steam or smoke. The flesh of the machine was raw and bloody. It sat on several legs, hidden in the shadow beneath its bulk. Jakk thought they might be stone.

Thin limbs emerged from various points on the machine's uneven body and lay limp across the ground. If they had once had a purpose it seemed that they were now redundant, or too weak to move. Some of them still bore skin, though most of it had peeled and died, littering the floor of the building with translucent flakes.

From the top of the machine came countless thick red veins. They were supported throughout the building by a network of timber braces and struts, and they all disappeared into vents and holes where the curved walls met the floor. The floor inside was lower than the ground level outside, and Jakk guessed that these pulsing veins passed below where he stood right now. He shifted his feet, uncomfortable at the thought.

"I've never seen anything like that," Rufiere said.

"It looks like a massive heart," Leeza said. "Or...."

"A brain," Barr said. He had spilled enough brains himself to know what they looked like. "Is that what you are?" he shouted, leaning into the hole and touching the machine with his shadow.

Its vents gushed steam for a beat, then it calmed again.

"Whatever it is, it's valuable enough for them to kill themselves over," Barr said. He looked back at the others, the tacky blood on his face almost black in the setting sun. "A living machine," he said. "One like no one's ever seen before."

"It's more than a machine," Jakk said. "We can't just take it."

Barr frowned. His eyes grew wider, madder in his mask of blood. "You've changed," he said.

Jakk shook his head. His heart was still tripping from the slaughter, and he could not hide the thrill he had felt at using his sword again. But he also felt desolate. "No," he said, "you have."

Barr snorted and shook his head, then turned back to the opening. "Keep watch," he said to Leeza. "I'll go and get it."

"Barr, please," Jakk said. "There's something more here, can't you sense it? They called it the heart and mind, and perhaps that's what it is. Maybe it runs this village, this valley, and if you take it away—"

"Keep watch, and shut him the fuck up." Barr climbed through the opening, and as he swung his sword before him the first of the veins split. They all heard the splash of fluid hitting the ground.

Leeza turned and stood with her back to the opening. Rufiere stood beside her, glancing nervously at Jakk.

"What, you're going to kill me now?" Jakk asked.

Leeza stared at him, her eyes giving away nothing.

"Going to kill me, when everything I say is true?"

Leeza smiled, and it was an expression he'd seen from her many times before. In a way he thought she was more dangerous even than Barr, because she did not have madness to blame.

Jakk stepped back, almost tripping over a body before he found bare ground. He was shaking. He felt eyes upon him, but wherever he looked he could only see the dead and dying.

He looked back at Leeza, tried to catch Rufiere's eyes, and then they all heard the sounds coming from inside the building. Barr's grunts first of all, and the splashes as more veins vented their contents across the ground. And then the hiss of steam, high-pitched whistles, the scrape of something metallic across stone.

The silent village gave voice to its agony. All around them came the sound of metal pipes vibrating, some throbbing so deeply that Jakk could feel them through the balls of his feet, others whistling, still more screeching so high that they went beyond hearing. It was a physical assault as well as aural, and Jakk felt his heart shaking in his chest. He feared it would burst.

Beneath the noise he heard people screaming.

Jakk clasped his hands over his ears and went to his knees. Rufiere and Leeza did the same, stumbling away from the bodies splayed around the building, grimacing as the noise sought to undo them.

As quickly as it had started screaming the village fell quiet again, but the noises continued from inside the invaded building. Jakk lowered his hands, and beneath the noise he could still hear screaming. This time it was only one voice.

The noise went on, Barr's screams continued, and then the venting started to stutter.

Barr appeared at the opening, glaring out into the fading light with something across his shoulder. It was one of the metallic pipes, still spewing steam as it tried to whistle, and Barr grabbed it with both hands as he stepped up and out of the building.

He dragged the machine with him. It pulsed and throbbed, trailing a forest of severed arteries behind it and leaving a smear of bloody fluid. Its pipes gushed steam and whistled softly, a sound in Jakk's ears that he feared would last forever.

The rest of the village was completely still and silent. No birds bothered the branches, and no flies worried at the dead.

"I have it!" Barr croaked, his voice failing. "I have it. Help me. Help me take it away."

Leeza went to help but Rufiere backed away, his gaze flitting back and forth between Jakk and the dying machine.

"It's nothing but a machine," Barr growled. But as he bumped it down a pile of bodies and started dragging it across the dusty ground, Jakk knew that he was so wrong.

———

BARR STRUGGLED through the village with the machine. It left a track of blood, and as Jakk followed he noticed scarlet points rising in the mess, pushing quickly up from the ground until they were almost up to his ankles. He hung back a little, watching the strange display. He did not actually see a blood rose bloom, but by the time Barr had pulled the machine from the village he knew what they were.

They saw no more of the villagers. Jakk did not understand that, but he was glad, because he was not sure whether he had any fight left in him. Perhaps there had been a final message to them in the machine's outpourings, or maybe they had already seen their own doom. He looked back at the village and was shocked to find that it looked no different. The trees were still tall and magnificent, the buildings randomly arranged either side of the river, and some of the metal chimneys still trickled steam. It almost looked as though he and the others had never even been there.

Barr groaned and shouted, falling down more and more as he dragged the heavy thing behind him. He refused to let anyone else help. "It's mine!" he shouted. "I took it, I suffered it, it's mine!"

Jakk was careful to avoid the smears of blood the thing left behind and the shoots that grew there, because he did not wish to touch or be touched by them. Perhaps his ideas were still informed by his time fighting in the Poison Forests, but infection was on his mind.

———

THEY ENDED up carrying Barr out of the valley. His prize had become too heavy, and blood had started seeping from his ears and eyes. Leeza claimed that he was dying. None of them were quite sure why. The three of them took turns supporting his weight as he walked, and when he could walk no more, they worked in shifts of two to carry him up the slopes towards the Noreela they knew.

They left Barr's machine by the side of the path. It seemed to have bled all of its blood along the road, and looking back in the fading light Jakk saw a slick of those stems growing still higher, supporting bulbous buds that would explode into blood roses when tomorrow came.

The edges of the valley seemed much steeper going up than they had coming down. It could have been that the mercenaries were exhausted from the fight and tired of carrying Barr now that he had started raving, or perhaps the darkness made the going that much harsher.

Or maybe, now that the folded valley had unfurled itself for them and what they brought, it was folding in once more.

They finished their journey in darkness, and when they finally reached the dying, fading plains of Noreela Jakk had never felt so at home.

THE FOUR folded people kneel beside his wife and child and breathe in whatever they take from the blooms. Then they stand and start to walk away. The woman who has been talking to him waits for him to follow, and Jakk begins. But leaving his family is not so easy. He pauses to look down at them, at how the morning sun streaks across their pale skin and the places where the roses sprout. There are wounds, but he hopes that they will heal. His wife's mouth is slightly open and a small beetle scurries across her chin, but when he reaches out to brush it away the woman steps close. He does not hear her footfalls.

"Leave them," she says.

"I can't."

"You will." She holds his arm and pulls him upright. Her fingers dig into his flesh, fingernails scratching his skin, and he looks back for as long as he can see Bindy and Romana. Even when they are obscured from view by trees and the lie of the land, still he looks at the tree canopy above where they lie.

Be safe, he thinks. *I'll come back to find you. Be safe.*

At last he turns to look the way they are walking. The woman lets go of his arm but stays close. Puffs of steam vent intermittently from the pipes placed in her shoulders and upper back. She does not blink, and her silvery eyes glint in the sun. But Jakk can see a boil on her chin, scratches on her arm, and close to her left eye there is a moon-shaped scar.

"What are you?" he asks.

"Children of the heart and mind."

"Is that all you're going to tell me?"

She looks at him, and for a beat she seems surprised. "That's all there is to tell."

She walks on ahead to join her companions, and for an instant he thinks of running. But they will be listening to him, perhaps smelling him. And she has already told him what happened to Rufiere and Leeza.

And what about Barr? he thinks. Since leaving the valley fifteen years before he has not seen or heard from his old fighting companions. They had parted ways upon leaving the valley, Jakk going north into Pengulfin Woods and the others suggesting they would head west towards Noreela City. Barr had been raving, bleeding, weak and close to death. Rufiere and Leeza said they'd try to save him, and when Jakk asked why they could not find a reasonable answer.

He left their company and they left his mind, and apart from the nightmares he has rarely thought about them since.

Yet Barr appeared before Jakk with a wound across his stomach and those roses blooming there, seeded by blood from the folded valley. Mad though he was back then it seems unlikely that the mercenary could have fought and escaped from these things.

"Did you send Barr to me?" he asks. The folded people keep walking as though they did not hear, steering awkwardly between the trees. "Hey!" Jakk shouts. Some birds take flight from above and something larger rustles through some undergrowth to his left.

The woman pauses and looks back. Her gaze chills him. She pulls back her sleeve and displays an open wound on her forearm. "He thought he escaped. We knew where he would go."

"You couldn't find me yourselves?" he asks. The woman turns and walks on, and there is something methodical and inhuman in her gait. She is simply doing what needs to be done, and her movements lack any hint of impulsiveness or curiosity.

But the pain she feels is obvious.

"We would have," she says at last. "Given time."

———

THEY WALK southeast through the forest, and Jakk recognises some of the places they pass by. He has hunted far and wide through Pengulfin Woods over the past fifteen years, and it feels more a part of him now than anywhere else on Noreela. The thought of travelling a landscape without trees is repellent and frightening. With so much wide open space, what is there to prevent him from tumbling across the world? At least here the trees keep him rooted. He touches the rough bark of one, the soft ginger trunk of another, and the woman-thing glances back as though she knows everything he does.

They march through the day, and when Jakk says he needs to stop and eat the woman catches a bird mid-flight and throws it back to him. He catches it, finds that it is still alive and drops it at his feet. The twitching, fluttering animal is quickly overrun by crown ants, the tiny creatures going for its eyes and beak and whistling softly as hundreds of them inject venom. The bird dies quickly. Jakk looks up to find the woman waiting for him, her companions moving on ahead.

"Not hungry anymore," Jakk says. She merely turns and starts walking again.

Jakk follows. They trail the scent of blood roses behind them, and now that smell is personal to him. *Romana and Bindy smell like that,* he thinks. He wonders what predators the smell could attract, both human and animal. His family calls to him, their hopelessness drawing him back, and the farther he walks the stronger the draw.

But if he runs, perhaps these things of the folded valley will kill him. It is not a chance he can take. Every moment he remains alive could be another beat closer to saving his wife and daughter.

"They're precious to me," he says. The woman holds back until she is walking by his side. He realises that he has not heard the other three things speak, and he wonders whether they are able, or whether they simply have nothing to say. "They're all I have, and you've done that to them. Imagine how that makes me feel."

"You're appealing to my emotions?" she asks.

"Do you have any?"

"They're not for the likes of you," she says, her tone of voice denying the statement. She does not look at him, and he wonders what her metallic eyes look like right now.

"Why haven't you looked for the valley yourselves?"

"We have. But the heart and mind didn't make us to return."

"Then why *did* it make you?"

"Only revenge."

"A machine that craves revenge?"

"It's much more than a machine," she says, and the statement does not surprise him because he knew it all along.

"And if you return, what will it do to you then?" Jakk is fascinated, both in the way this thing moves and talks, and the reasons it has for being here.

"Perhaps it will welcome us back."

"To your family?" Jakk asks.

The woman is silent for a long while, the only sound her soft footfalls and an occasional whisper of steam from her pipes. Then she turns to Jakk and he is shocked by the expression on her face. Hatred. "They were precious to me," she says. "And I was five years old when I saw them slaughtered."

"Slaughtered?" But he already knows what she means. It was a small village, after all.

"The one you called Barr killed my father. My brother died three days later from his wounds, giving his strength to comfort the injured heart and mind. My mother...you. A knife. Her belly." She walks on quickly, barges through a thicket of ferns and kicks out at a fallen branch. The wood splinters beneath her foot.

The other folded people do not even glance back.

———

JAKK ASKS no more. They look like machines clothed in the flesh of humans, yet the woman now acts like a human implanted with the facets of a machine. He does not wish to challenge her identity further, because the more he observes them, the more scared he becomes.

He knows he does not deserve happiness, but with his family taken from him he is craving what is lost.

They walk until sundown. With dusk comes the wildlife of the forest: wood wolves howling at the stars, foxlions slipping from shadow to shadow, and red bears sharpening their claws on the bones of unwary travellers. Normally Jakk and his family would be secure in their home, or if he was on a long hunting trip he would be hidden safely in a tree, but now the folded people keep walking. Jakk hurries to keep up, trying to walk with a couple of them on each side. Either they do not know the dangers or they are not scared.

They do not stop for food or sleep. Jakk is strong and he keeps up, but several times his stomach rumbles noisily, and once or twice his thoughts go back to that bird he gave to the ants.

Their steam pipes sing more often in the darkness. They whistle and hum, and by the time dawn smears the horizon and they emerge from the southern extreme of the Pengulfin Woods, the folded people are walking more awkwardly, no longer possessing even a trace of the grace of machines. The exhaust from the pipes is sometimes a dirty brown colour instead of white or pink. Their eyes are dulled and tarnished.

"You seem tired," Jakk says.

The woman shakes her head. None of them have spoken for a long time, and she seems unwilling to break her silence.

She reaches into a pocket in her long coat, brings something out and throws it at Jakk. He recognises it instantly. It is Rufiere's leather-bound book, the volume he always claimed to be a Book of Ways. He glances at the woman, then opens the book and flips through the thick silk-grass pages. They are tattered along their edges, faded with time, and the top corner of each page is stained with blood.

"He tried to show," she says. Her voice sounds different, and Jakk realises there is a very human weakness to it now. "But we've followed, and he showed wrong."

Jakk turns page after page. He has never travelled far, and he does not know whether the maps and comments are accurate or fanciful. But when he finds a page scored deep with a fresh dark line of charcoal he stops. On the bottom of the map, to the south, are the northern borders of the Ventgorian Steam Plains. At the top, marked with a score of tiny trees, lies the southern edge of the Pengulfin Woods. In between Rufiere has marked the folded valley with a thick finger-shaped line. He has gone over it again and again to make it never disappears.

Jakk looks up. "We're not there yet," he says.

"You know where he was wrong?" the woman asks.

"Of course," Jakk says. *No*, he thinks. *I haven't a fucking clue. I was a mercenary, not a map maker.*

"Show us."

He steps forward with the book held out, finger pointing to some arbitrary area east of where Rufiere tried to score the valley into existence.

"No," the woman says. "*Show* us."

Jakk nods and starts walking, and this time it is they who follow him.

HE HEARS them talking. The woman first, her voice low and slow, and then the others join in. He cannot hear the words, but as the day wears on and they draw closer to where the valley almost certainly will not be, Jakk knows that they are becoming desperate.

I should go, he thinks. He has looked behind several times now, and every time he turns around they seem less organised and weaker. The only time one of them raises a voice it is the woman, responding to some muttered entreaty.

"No more!" she says. "We're going back."

But they are not going back. Because the valley is closed to them, and the heart and mind sent them out for vengeance, and vengeance only. And if Jakk knows and understands that, he wonders why they cannot.

THEY STOP beside a huge old machine, a metallic construct that still has the leathery remnants of its biological parts flapping in the breeze, hardened through its core and stretched impossibly thin across rusted domes. The folded people stare at it for a long time, their steam vents hissing, and when they finally sit down and lean against it they seem to forget that Jakk is even there. He waits for a while, standing still as a stone while the things converse in pained whispers, then he turns and walks away. If they are readying to kill him now is the time. It must surely be obvious to them that their creator is not about to welcome them back.

So he will die or escape, and he has little control over what will be. Weaker though they seem, he cannot fight them. He can't find the folded valley that is no longer there. The further they walked, the more he thought about Rufiere's solid black line, and how the dead mercenary would have been very particular and exact about where he drew it.

The folded people do not follow. He does not believe that they let him go, but abandoned by their maker they have simply stopped caring. And even after what they did to his family, Jakk can't help but wonder what will become of them. They could remain here and rot against the old dead machine, or perhaps they will rise again and continue looking, catching the occasional unwary traveller to seed with their blood roses so that they can draw power from the living again. Maybe they will never die.

Perhaps one day the folded valley will open to them again. He will never know.

———

HE HAS to eat. Lacking any weapons, unsure of whether there are any farms or villages close by, he sets about making a snare. He peels bark into thin strips, ties the lengths into a rope, bends and secures a sapling, positions the loop and retreats behind a small clump of trees to await his prey. And every beat he spends waiting to catch his food, he thinks of Romana and Bindy. What they mean to him, how they look, how they smell, the lengths he would go to protect them, and what he would do if anything ever happened to them. He has seen and caused so much death in his life that, selfishly, he hopes that of the three of them he will die first. He knows that will leave them to suffer and grieve, but now that he has such goodness in his life he knows that losing it would kill him.

A rabbit trips the snare, and soon he is cooking it over a roaring fire.

The smell attracts a small group of skull ravens. They roost on a tree a hundred steps from where he eats, and he throws stones at them as he chews on the rabbit's leg. They do not fly away, and he remembers the last time he threw stones at such birds. Then, he was interrupted by the smell of blood roses drifting on the breeze. Now there is nothing but the odour of cooking meat. He moves upwind from the fire and breathes in again, but the rabbit grease is on his breath.

He moves on, leaving the remains of the rabbit and the skull ravens behind. The birds ignore the meat and watch him go.

———

JAKK REACHES the forest, passes through and steers unerringly to where they stole him away from his family. He smells the blood roses from a distance, that meaty scent inspiring a hundred bad memories. *My mother...you. A knife. Her belly.* The folded woman's words come back to him, but try as he might he cannot remember the killing she described. There were so many in the valley that they all blurred into one.

"I'm sorry," he says to the breeze as he starts to run. The smell grows stronger. He is going the right way, because he knows these woods as well as his wife's smile and his daughter's laughter.

His apology serves no purpose, and he's not entirely sure he means it.

He sees a flash of red in the distance and stops. *What if they're dead?* He cannot allow that thought. Not here, not this close. He starts running again, faster than he has run for a long time, and soon the spread of blood roses appears before him.

This is the place. He recognises the lightning-struck wellburr tree to his left, the small rocky outcropping from the hillside to his right, the way the trees are spaced, the afternoon light splaying shadows across the ground, but Bindy and Romana are not here.

They are not here.

He walks slowly through the roses until he reaches the place where he remembers his wife lying. And Romana was over there to his left....

They are not here.

This is where the roses grow thickest, where his wife and daughter should be. There are two dense groupings of the plants, the odour rich, the sap dripping with a sound that seems to reverberate through the forest. As he steps back, he sees the distinct shapes these clumps of roses form.

He sits with his back against a tree and cries.

"Maybe they'll come back," he says. The words have no power, and neither do his tears, but he cannot stop talking to himself and crying.

The sun goes down and Jakk still cannot move. He stays there and listens to the furtive night sounds of the forest. And as he breathes in the heavy, heady scent of the folded valley, he knows what is to come. ◦—

THE BAJUMAN

1

MY EYES were burning again, so I sucked in another lungful of ants. As ever, the sensation was only unpleasant for the first few heartbeats. Then the ants stopped scuttling, my eyes stopped burning, and all the bad parts of my life faded away.

I liked to let the rush guide itself. I closed my eyes and saw things that had never happened play out across my crimson vision. The familiar sense of unbelonging faded, and everyone who walked the streets outside was aware of me, my place in the world, my worth. The knife wound in my left thigh from several years ago ceased aching. Gone was the time I sat and watched my father dying from the grot-plague, and here was an image of the two of us beside a lake on the Cantrass Plains; we were fishing and laughing, and he loved and respected me then as he never had for real. My eyelids lightened as the sun emerged from behind a cloud, and as the effect of the ants' dying breaths began to fade, my father's eyes turned black and his skin began to pale.

"Bajuman! Someone to see you."

I groaned and sat up, wiping a couple of rogue ants from my chin. Shelya saw—she always saw—but she grunted and looked away, and left the door to my room open as she descended the creaking stairs. She saw, but she didn't care.

I made sure the lid was screwed tightly onto the ant pot, gauze in place to allow them to breathe. I'd dropped a grub in yesterday and they were still working at it, slicing off parts of its body, slicing again, reducing their food to mouth-sized chunks. I thought the grub moved slightly, though it could have been the vibration as I swung off the bed.

I held my head. It hurt. Two bottles of rotwine and an evening of gush ants would do that to a person.

"Who is it?" I called. I heard a pause in the movement from below, but Shelya did not reply. My rent money was good enough for her, but she only spoke to me if it was absolutely necessary. The pause ended and the rattle of bottles began again. There would be people in her small tavern again tonight, drinking and eating and telling each other that someone else was dead. I often sat up here and listened. Information was a large part of my job, and the realisation that these people actually seemed to miss the trials and horrors of the Great Plagues made me feel better about myself. I'd spent many years coming to terms with the fact that I was as good as anyone, and better than some, but being Bajuman left its scar.

I felt a tickling on my cheek and plucked the last ant from my skin. It struggled between my fingers, waving its antennae at the air, and I studied it closely. Strange, that a little creature like this could have such an effect. I placed it on my tongue and closed my mouth.

My room was small and functional, but comfortable enough to call home. A bed, a cupboard for my clothes and shoes, a chair and desk, a small shelf piled with books, and a partitioned area in the corner for toilet and washing. I had an old rug on the floor supposedly woven by Cantrass Angels—

payment from one of my clients—and though threadbare and dusty, it retained its brilliant colours as though made only yesterday. It gave the grey room a much-needed vibrancy. I stood on the rug and dressed, hiding my knives, short sword and crossbow beneath my long coat. Then I closed my eyes and sighed, trying to forget the gush ants and ready myself for cruel reality.

Someone to see you, Shelya had said. None of my few friends ever visited me here. Which meant that this was either a new client seeking my services, or someone come to kill me.

———

I WENT down the narrow back stairs, passed Shelya in the kitchen—she didn't even acknowledge me—and slipped from the back door. Something squealed and scurried away along the alley. Something else growled and chomped, and the squeal ended.

The alley stank, and it wasn't much better when I emerged onto the main street. I looked left and right, trying to spot shapes hiding in shadows, but I saw only the usual whores and dealers. I nodded a brief greeting to some. A man ran by, hands flapping around his head, and I closed my hand around my sword's handle. But no one and nothing followed.

I turned right and leaned close to the first window of Shelya's tavern. The place had no name, but the small sign above her front door told everyone what they needed to know. It showed a splayed hand with the middle finger missing, fingertips painted red. *Come here to drink, but bring your own mugs.* It was an ironic dig against the militia who, until the Great Plagues had faded to an end a couple of years before, had cut a finger from anyone found sharing drinking vessels in taverns or food halls. Having endured the last of the Plagues, many people now struggled to survive with only a finger or two on each hand.

There was only one person in the tavern. The woman sat at a table with her back to the door. She wore a heavy leather coat, hood lined with a type of fur I'd never seen before, and as she closed a hand around her glass I saw gems twinkling on her fingers. So, she had money. One good sign. If she was a client she could pay, and it was usually only people as low as, or lower than me who would bother to want me dead. One of the few blessings of being Bajuman.

The woman drained her glass of rotwine and refilled it from the bottle Shelya had left. I was tempted to wait here and watch this woman get drunk, but something told me I'd be waiting a long time. I was sure she could afford much better that rotwine, but she seemed to be enjoying the rancid drink nonetheless.

I opened the door and barged in, hand hovering low so that I could pull a knife if needed. "Does that fucking Bajuman live here?" I roared. The woman turned in her seat, eyes wide and scared, and I stared her down.

Shelya dashed from the kitchen hefting a carving knife, but her shoulders dropped when she saw me standing there. "It's you," she said. She pointed at the woman with the knife, as if unaware that the rest of the tavern was filled with empty chairs. "There she is."

"So I see."

"You're Korrin?" the seated woman said.

I eyed her up and down, enjoying her discomfort. There was something about her I didn't like, but I could not yet place it. Strange, for me. Reading people was much of my job, and it had saved my life on numerous occasions.

She didn't seem to be looking down on me. That didn't make me as comfortable as it should.

"Who's asking?" I said.

She stood, hands clasped before her stomach. She bore no weapons that I could see. In this neighbourhood, for someone carrying the goods she wore, that was brave or stupid. This woman looked neither. "My name is Rhyl Santon," she said. "I come from the Northern Districts."

"I could have told you that," I said.

She smiled, reinforcing the something I didn't like. Even though I still didn't know what that something was. "What else can you tell?" she asked.

"A test?"

She inclined her head, shrugged. Her lips were darkened with rotwine, but she did not appear drunk. I suddenly had a craving for a glass myself. I stepped past her and emptied the bottle into her glass, took a long draught, smacked my lips together.

"You should lose a finger for that," she said.

I showed her my hands. "Full complement." I looked her up and down again, examined the coat and the fur I did not recognise, the gems on her fingers—small, so probably expensive—the intricate tattoos that circled her neck and disappeared below her high-cut dress. "So, you want to know about yourself. Well, you're rich."

"Well observed." The sarcasm did not change her face.

"You're travelled. You've been to Long Marrakash. You like to have more than people know about, and you approach every conversation from a position of power. And that tattoo that runs down from your neck does not touch your breasts." I glanced down, then up at her face. A small, uncomfortable smile played there, and I knew I was right on target so far. Now for the killing stroke. "You're married. You use rhellim one evening in two, and prefer to make your husband lie down while you ride him."

"How do you know that?"

"Lucky guess." I stared at her chest for longer than was necessary and felt a moment of satisfaction when she started to fidget.

"You're Bajuman," she said, and I smiled, because they all tried to play my own game. "Nobody likes you, and you're only tolerated because no one can be bothered to hunt you all down and banish you from Noreela City."

I sat in the chair she had been using, smiled, clapped my hands lightly together, and realised that perhaps I liked this Rhyl Santon after all. The thing bothering me about her had resolved itself in her last statement; she was a fair woman, but she hated showing that. I guessed that in her circles, that would have been seen as a weakness.

"You don't mind that I'm Bajuman," I said. "I appreciate that. Would you like some more rotwine?"

She paused only for a heartbeat, then smiled. "Not everyone needs to live to old prejudices." She sat opposite me and relaxed. The strain went from her face and her shoulders fell. She tapped her fingernails on the scored tabletop as though trying to read the countless names carved there.

"I charge ten tellans per day," I said. "That's the basic. Once you've told me how I can help you, that may change."

"Depending on how dangerous it may be?"

"Or how interesting."

"Oh."

Shelya must have been listening to our conversation. She came in with another open bottle of rotwine, smiling at Rhyl Santon and ignoring me completely. "Can I get you some food?" she asked.

"No, thank you."

"*I'd* like some," I said. Shelya walked back to the kitchen, sniffing thickly as she passed from view.

"Will she bring you anything?" Rhyl asked.

"No."

"But she lets you live here?"

"I pay. Bajuman money is the same as anyone else's."

Her head tilted and her lips pursed, and I knew what was coming.

"Don't pity me, rich woman," I said.

Rhyl turned away. "I'm sorry."

"Don't be. I'm strong. I find hate easier to deal with than pity." I poured the wine—Shelya had brought two glasses, at least—and sat back in the chair. It crackled and groaned, and I laced my fingers behind my head. "So, how can I be of service?"

"First, you come highly recommended. I asked five people I know—friends, acquaintances—who could help me in this matter, and three of them gave your name. They know of you through reputation, I believe. They say you can get things done quickly and...quietly."

"The advantage of being untouchable is that nobody sees or notices you. It helps me hear things, see things, get places."

"Do you only work in the City?"

"Mostly. I once did some work in the Widow's Peaks, but it's too wild for my liking. I like my luxuries." I sipped more wine and thought of the dead ants melting away in my stomach.

"I need you to find someone for me," Rhyl said.

"Missing person." I looked away from Rhyl and sniffed for cooking food. *Well, she's already up to fifteen per day,* I thought. Noreela City was a city of missing people, and finding one was like finding one particular sewer rat. A true challenge.

"Not missing," she said. "Taken. Stolen. Kidnapped." For the first time there was a break in her voice, and I looked in time to see her touching her left eye.

"Someone close to you?"

"A friend."

"You haven't been to the militia?"

Her eyes widened. "You think they'd help?"

"You're monied. You're *decent.*"

"Mage-shit, they're just as likely to be the ones who've taken him."

"Him?"

Rhyl nodded. "Do you want to write down the details?"

I tapped the side of my head. "Keep it all up here. That way, no one can take it."

"Very well." Rhyl stood and paced the tavern for a few beats, finishing at the window through which I had first seen her. She rubbed greasy grime from the glass and looked out onto the street. Lanterns were being lit now, and reflected flames danced across her features. Was she smiling? Crying? I could not tell. Only a small mystery in my life full of many, but it was important that I knew.

"His name is Fod Larima."

I kept my surprise to myself. *Fodder!*

"He is a friend of mine and my husband's. We took him in three years ago, and three days ago someone stole him from our house."

"Stole?"

Rhyl glanced at me and away again, flustered. "Kidnapped," she said. "They came over the wall and forced open a downstairs window. Larima was asleep. We found a few small bloodstains, but no signs of a struggle, so we assume they struck him over the head and carried him away. Must have been at least two of them. Like all fodder, Larima is a big man."

I nodded and closed my eyes, trying not to act too surprised. By the Black this was interesting! But it was also, I was already certain, quite hopeless.

"You do know that he's probably been eaten by now, don't you?"

Rhyl began to cry, and this time she did not try to hide her tears. She was either very good, or they were completely genuine. I went with genuine, and turned away.

"Please," she said, "you don't need to do that. It's no shame."

"Forgive me," I said. "Like all Bajumans, I'm used to averting my eyes." *And making someone uncomfortable is the easy way to their truths*, I thought.

"I can't believe that's happened to him. Not Larima. I'm not *able* to believe it. He's so intelligent, and loving, and such a good friend to us. How could *anyone!*"

"There are still those who eat fodder as a delicacy," I said. "And others—a few—who still regard eating them as their birthright."

"How could anyone?" Rhyl said, quieter.

"Sit down," I said. "Let's have another drink. Tell me everything you know, answer my questions, and I'll do the best I can."

"You're taking it on?" she said, delight cutting through her tears.

"Of course. You're rich, and you'll pay well."

Rhyl nodded, dabbed at her eyes. "And, of course, it's an interesting case."

I nodded and smiled.

Rhyl sat down and took a drink of rotwine without flinching, then upended her glass and crunched it down onto the table in the customary deal-done sign. This gesture was so far below her social circle that I was slightly taken aback, but I finished my glass and did the same. Neither of us bled from the smashed glasses; a good sign.

"You'll find him," she said. ⌒

7

I WAITED in my room, sharpening knives and filling a clip with crossbow bolts.

I'll pay you thirty tellans per day, not ten, Rhyl Santon had said at the end of our discussion, *but you'll be taking someone with you.*

I work alone, I had replied.

You work with this man, or you don't work at all.

It had not been a threat. Even as I nodded and accepted the conditions, I had convinced myself of that. Not a threat at all. Simply a statement that, had I not agreed to this company, Rhyl Santon would have taken her business elsewhere. *Not a physical threat against me,* I thought. *She doesn't work like that.*

I finished sharpening my knives and choosing a dozen bolts, and when that was done I stood by the window and looked down into the alley between buildings. As ever, there were shadows moving down there. Noreela City by night was as dangerous as anywhere else in Noreela. I was a part of this night life; it was where I did my best work. Things in the dark wished to remain unseen, and the unseen hoarded secrets like a witch amasses false charms. By day the City's trade was in goods. By night, it dealt in information.

I'd lived here for most of my forty years. Many people recognised me as a Bajuman, and that was harsh. But I had heard many stories about what was happening beyond the city walls, how the land itself had changed and was winding down since the Cataclysmic War over two centuries before. That was harsher. I'd take hateful stares over volcanic eruptions any day.

I caught a whiff of rot and closed the window. Sometimes the city still stank of death, as though the corpses of half a million Great Plagues victims still burnt on the plains beyond the city walls. I thought of my father, fading away with the grot-plague, and I turned and looked at the jar of ants.

There was a thump at the door and it drifted open with its latch broken. A huge man stood there, so tall that I could only see the bottom half of his face below the doorframe. He was wide enough to shut out candlelight from the landing, and when he bent to enter the room his jacket stretched across his muscled chest. His scalp was bald, and scarred with a dozen patches of pale yellow skin. A plague survivor. I went to pull a knife but he was across the room faster than I could blink. I didn't ever hear the creak of floorboards.

He grabbed me by the throat and pressed me against the window. I heard the snick of a glass pane cracking, and it reminded me of the upended deal-sealing glasses.

"I don't like Bajumans," he whispered. His breath settled across my face and made me gag; he smelled as though he was rotting from the inside out.

"I don't like bad breath," I wheezed.

He pushed harder, lifting me higher and cracking my head against the lintel. "I *mean* it," he said. "I'm here because Mistress Santon requests it. You're my guide, and little else. On any normal day...." He hawked and spat a viscous gob onto my stomach. "On any normal day, I'd rather talk to a lump of sheebok shit than a Bajuman." He dropped me, stepped back and started wiping his hand. He sniffed it. "You smell *worse* than sheebok shit!" he said. He held his hand away from his body as though it was contaminated.

I smelled better than him, I knew that for a fact. I touched my throat and breathed in and out a few times, hoping it would not bruise too much. "Glad to hear you're as enlightened as your Mistress," I said.

"She makes her own choices," the man said. "I serve her, not her opinions."

I sat down on my bed and held my head in my hands. "Well then, we're off to a good start."

"I don't want to be here, Bajuman."

"How strange, I don't want you here either."

"I could rip your head off with one hand and play with myself with the other."

I nodded and looked up at the huge man. "And that, I suspect, is why you don't feel the need to read."

He grunted. I wasn't sure he quite understood. I thought I could probably reach the short knife in my belt—probably—before he got to me, but he turned and left the room as quickly and quietly as he had entered. I had to admire his stealth for such a big man. But I'd never say it aloud.

"Tomorrow," he growled. "I'll be here at sunup. Be ready."

"I'm ready now," I said. "I work mainly at night. That way, fewer people have to look at me. I hope you didn't have a prior engagement." I cringed, pushed my way out past the man, then turned and tried to secure my door. The catch was cracked, the wood around it splintered. At least few would lower themselves to steal from me.

"My name's Korrin," I said. I looked up at the man, holding his gaze. "If we're to work together, at least tell me your name."

"We're not working together," he said.

"Your name?"

He turned and descended toward Sheyla's tavern. I sighed and followed. It was going to be a long night.

I LEFT Sheyla's and turned right, heading south toward the city wall. Five minutes' walking would take me there. I felt the presence of the big man behind me, holding back so that it did not seem that we were together. He was a thug and probably a killer, yet he worried enough about his image to not be seen with a Bajuman. Perhaps that would serve me well if things turned bad.

"Keep up," I said over my shoulder. I did not turn to see his expression. *If it weren't for his Mistress, he'd probably slip a knife between my shoulder blades right now.* I wondered whether he had ever killed a Bajuman. The thought drove rotwine from my system and silenced any more quips.

A group of women passed us, heading in the opposite direction. They were all dressed in yellow, hoods raised over their heads, arms folded across their chests as they walked. Some of them whispered, but their voices died out as they drew level with us.

"Good evening," I said, pausing to press my hand to my chest.

One of the women glanced up, evidently surprised. "Show me the good," she said. Her voice sounded as if she was gargling filthy river water.

The plague survivors passed me by. As they reached Santon's thug they began whispering again. He stepped back to let them pass, but I saw something other than disgust on his face. He looked at me and frowned, trying to appear threatening once more.

"We're all survivors," I said. "We just survive different things."

"I can accept philosophising from Mistress Santon," he said. "But you shut the fuck up."

I shook my head and turned away. By the Black, this really was going to be a long night.

———

AS WE approached the city wall we came across the first group of militia. There were six of them sitting around a large table. The table was heavy with bottles of rotwine and jugs of ale, swords and throwing knives, plates of meat and vegetables steaming into the night. A man and woman hurried from a nearby building and placed two more plates on the table. One of the militia mumbled his thanks and reached for another chunk of meat.

The street was narrow here, buildings high and looming on both sides, and well-lit with oil lamps. The militia's table all but blocked the street. They were, I supposed, on guard.

"We need to go around," I said. "They're drunk, and they may detain us for fun."

"Where are we heading?" the big man asked.

"A whorehouse close to the city's southern gate."

He stared over my head at the feasting militia, not questioning our destination. "Every beat we waste takes Larima closer to death," he said. He grinned down at me, revealing teeth that reflected the yellow of the death moon. "Don't follow too closely, Bajuman."

Santon's man moved around me and approached the militia. I sighed, closed my eyes and listened for the first signs of trouble. I heard laughter instead.

I watched one of the militia stand at the man's approach, but he appeared at ease. His sword remained on the table, and his hands still bore food and drink.

The laughter came from Santon's man.

"So you fight crime by eating stolen food now, Koop?"

The militia chewed slowly, taking his time. "What makes you think it's stolen, Jammer?"

Jammer—at least now I had a name—used the opportunity to survey the feast. The silence was suddenly loaded; no more laughter. *Where is this going?* I thought. I glanced to my right, marking a narrow alley that led between buildings and towards the city wall two streets to the south. If I had to make a break for it, that was my route.

"To begin with," Jammer said, "*you're* eating it, Koop. You never ate militia food if there was something better going." The man and woman darted from the house again, carrying more food-laden plates. "Catch you smuggling, did he?" Jammer asked the woman. She glanced nervously at the standing militia, slid her plate onto the table, then disappeared back into the house.

Koop shrugged. "Seemed a shame to let such quality contraband go to rot," he said. "Care to join us?" He glanced past Jammer, acknowledging my presence for the first time. "You and your friend?"

"He's not a friend," Jammer said quietly. "I'm on a job."

"Ah, more work for the rich mistress." Koop sat down, nodded, picked up a bottle of rotwine. "Twenty tellans says I never saw you."

Jammer drew a bag of coins from his pocket and dropped a handful onto the plate in front of Koop. Some tinkled, but most pattered down onto meat and cooling vegetables.

"Enjoy your meal," he said. Then he glanced back at me and walked past the militia.

I followed, trying to appear nonchalant. The smell of the food was very good. I guessed it was stolen from the farms that served the Northern Districts; good meat, well fed.

Koop glanced at me, but that was all.

Jammer was waiting for me around the next corner. His face was hard, lips pressed tight. I asked no questions.

"This way," I said, walking on.

No, no questions. I had seen enough. ✑

3

AS I had already guessed, Jammer seemed to know the brothel I was heading for. He followed me along the street, through the narrow alley and into the shadow of the city wall, and when I approached the brothel's entrance he held back. He mumbled something about "checking out the area", as though he could possibly find some clue to Larima's whereabouts on the dark city streets. I nodded and carried on.

The building housing the brothel was three storeys high. The city wall stood behind it, strong and impassive, and the darkness gave it the impression of leaning in. I felt a moment of dizziness. I shook my head and put my left hand in my pocket, gripping the handle of the small crossbow slung from my belt. If the dark alleys and streets bore trouble through Noreela City like veins, then this brothel would be its heart.

Which was exactly the reason why I had decided to come here first. I knew this place better than most; its construction, its history, the way it was run. And sex was only one commodity bought and sold here.

The door was set back in the wall, hidden in permanent shadow. Old machine parts had been cast into the stone blocks around the door, presenting a sharp metallic façade. I rapped on one curved metal shell and waited for the door to open.

Jammer was hiding in the mouth of an alley thirty steps away. I had heard him pause there, his breath fast and light. I could not decide whether he was afraid or excited.

The door clicked and clunked as bolts were drawn. The first thing through was a sword, lifting my chin so that its bearer could see my face.

"What'll you want?" the doorman said. I didn't recognise him—I had not visited for over a year—but the brothel had a fast turnover of staff. Its owner, though...she had been here forever.

"I want to see Madone," I said.

For a long time the doorman said nothing. The tip of the sword remained pressed into the underside of my chin, causing me to rise slightly onto my toes. It was starting to hurt.

"Check him, please," the doorman said at last.

Something shimmered in the air before me. A woman appeared from the shadows, gorgeous and somehow terrible, with deep black eyes and hair tied into four tails that snaked down her body. She wore a thin dress that moulded to every curve. Even in the shadows I could see the outline of her heavy breasts, wide hips, strong shoulders. *Cantrass Angel*! I had no idea the Madone had gone so up-market.

The Angel stood before me and leaned in close, nudging the doorman's sword away with one shoulder. She was short, so she had to rise up on her toes, but she moved with grace and ease. She breathed in my breath and smiled, eyes twinkling with reflected life-moonlight.

"Come for something special?" she whispered. Her accent was strange and exotic, her breath rich with the tang of something more seductive than mere sex.

"A talk with Madone," I whispered back. She touched my shoulders, chest, stomach, and when her hand brushed against my hard cock she smiled.

"Surely something more?"

I closed my eyes and returned the smile. "Perhaps another day," I said.

"Oh, I'm sure." Her tongue flickered out and touched my lips. *Those Cantrass Angels*, I had once heard Madone say. *They know so much more. Almost as if they've had eternity to learn it.* I opened my eyes and watched the Angel step backward through the door.

"Allow him in."

The guard stepped aside. I adjusted myself, kept my grip on the crossbow, and entered the brothel.

The Cantrass Angel had already disappeared. I stood in the same wide, well-lit hallway I remembered from my previous visits, though now the walls were slung with weavings and tapestries. A hundred burning candles imbued the air with a spicy tang. At the hallway's centre stood a round fountain, and a small sheebok walked a continuous circuit around its stone ledge, working the mechanism that drew water. I had once asked Madone why they went to such great lengths to keep the fountain working. She had touched the sheebok and paused its movement, and the sounds of sex came from all around. *I value my clients' privacy*, she had said, nudging the creature once more.

I had laughed then, and I smiled now. Such double standards were why Madone had often been one of my first calls in a new case.

As if thinking of her could conjure her presence, Madone emerged through the beaded curtains at the rear of the hall. She looked me up and down, gaze resting on my concealed left hand. "Oh, Korrin," she said, "please tell me you've come here for a fuck."

"I see you have some new girls."

"Oh, you've met one of the Angels! Aren't they wonderful? I thought someone like you would have heard about them."

"Perhaps the word has yet to spread."

"Strange girls," Madone said. "They make everyone feel special, so no one talks about them. When you fuck an Angel, you think you're the only one for them, forever."

I thought of the woman drawing in my breath, her dark eyes gleaming. "Tempting," I said.

Madone sat on the edge of the fountain and the sheebok nudged against her thigh, pausing in its incessant circling. As the sound of flowing water faded away, so the echoes of sex came in. "I can arrange for you to meet one in private," Madone said.

"Tempting," I said again. "But you know me...."

"Always working." Madone frowned. "Alone?"

I knew better than to lie to Madone. She had eyes everywhere, especially here. "A client sent her thug with me," I said. "He's outside. Didn't want to come in."

"Name?"

"Jammer. Ex-militia."

Madone's face darkened and she looked down at the creature panting against her leg. "Indeed," she said. "So you're working for rich people now, Korrin?"

"They pay well. And the case is interesting."

"What are you after this time?"

I sat beside Madone and looked around. There was obviously history between her and Jammer, but now was not the time to probe. I was here for information about the missing fodder, not the mercenary.

"Can I ask you and the watcher at the same time?"

Madone sat up straight, feigning offence. "What makes you think I'll help you?"

I smiled.

THE WATCHER lived in a room at the centre of the brothel. Like most of the rooms it was windowless, but the walls were holed in scores of places, each one hiding shadows. I knew that these holes connected to corridors, rooms and doorways throughout the building. In the centre, a bed. On the bed, the watcher.

"Usual price," Madone said. I nodded.

The watcher seemed to be asleep, but I knew otherwise. She was naked, and her yellow skin glistened with beads of dusty sweat. Her eyes moved beneath closed eyelids. On a table beside the bed sat a glass bowl filled with fledge. I could smell the drug from the doorway, and I knew it was stale. It seemed that Madone could afford drapes and decoration, but not yet fresh fledge.

It was from this room that Madone made the bulk of her money. The brothel was a tool for harvesting information. Before me on the bed lay the harvester.

The fledger's eyes opened and she sat up, panting. Sweat dribbled down her body and soaked into the sheet at her waist. She made no attempt to cover herself. She smiled at Madone.

"Busy day," Madone said.

The fledger nodded. "You should send Jay in soon. I've read so much, I'm afraid some of it will slip away."

"Korrin is here to ask you something first," Madone said.

I had been here before. I knew how this went. Even so, I never failed to find it an unpleasant experience. I had tried to convince myself that what Madone and the fledger did here harmed no one. But it was theft, pure and simple; theft of thoughts and dreams. Stealing from a mind while its owner had sex seemed low, yet it had helped me solve several cases in the past.

"I'm looking for someone named Fod Larima," I said.

"A fodder?" Madone said.

I nodded. "He's a friend of my client. He was kidnapped, and she wants him back before any harm comes to him."

"Before he's eaten, you mean?" The fledger was almost smiling. I hated her yellow eyes. They seemed so animal.

"Before any harm comes to him."

The fledger frowned and looked away, concentrating. "When was he taken?"

"Three days ago." I glanced up at the shelves that lined one wall of the room, and the hundreds of thick books sitting there. Most of the spines were marked with days, years and moon-spans, and those on the highest shelves went back decades. As always, I tried to imagine what secrets were contained in their pages. It was quite possible that these books were priceless, and almost certainly deadly in the wrong hands. Their secrets could cause leaders to fall, races to rise, wars to begin and ages to end. And yet, even though the blackmail potential must be huge, Madone only sold information that was asked for. It was a strange moral code, but it gave me some form of comfort.

I wondered whether my name was written on any of those pages.

"I won't need those," the fledger said, seeing me eyeing her journals. "There's one mention I can recall from the last three days. May be your fodder, may not. A trader came down from the Northern Districts on business, dealing with wine merchants from Ventgoria. He visits here each time he's away from home. He has a wife, but.... Well, she doesn't do what he wants. One of our whores from the south does, if he pays her well enough. She doesn't like it. He knows that, and he talks inconsequentialities while he shafts, and this time he told her he was procuring wine for a dinner party. As he fucked, he was imagining eating forbidden food."

"Fodder?"

"I don't know." The fledger shook her head, glanced at her wall of books. "For him it's still a mystery party, with the promise of forbidden things."

"Do you have a name?"

"His name is Morton. That's all I've ever known him by. He's not a...good man." The fledger closed her eyes, as though touching his mind again.

"Can you tell me how long ago this was?" I asked.

The fledger spoke without opening her eyes. "Half a day. It may be that Morton is still in the Southern Districts. I believe a train of wine traders came in from Ventgoria two days ago."

I knew better than to ask her to probe out for him now. Though this fledger sat at the centre of the brothel and provided Madone with her true income, still she was weak and sick from stale fledge. The many holes in the walls provided routes through which her floating mind could travel and observe. They made it easier for her. Without the holes, she would probably never be able to leave the room.

And yet....

"There's a man, sent to accompany me by my employer." Madone glanced sharply at me but I pretended not to notice. I guessed I had a few beats more before being thrown out. "His name is Jammer, and he refused to come in here with me. Can you tell me why?"

The fledger's eyes snapped open and she drew back on the bed, pulling the sheet up to cover her bare breasts.

"Time to go," Madone said. "You can pay me outside."

"Jammer?" I said.

"Don't ask me to touch his mind," the fledger said. She reached into the glass bowl and pulled out a thumb of the drug, chewing into it as Madone hustled me from the room.

"What in the Black was that?" she hissed.

I smiled, but Madone was genuinely angry. "I'm sorry," I said. "But with this man at my back for the next few days, I want to know about him."

"He's bad, Korrin. Not bad like the thieves that work the markets, or the druggers that come up from the south with wares that kill. *Really* bad. He won't come in here because of what he did last time, when he was militia. The girl still has her scars. She screams herself awake every morning, and she hasn't worked since. She hasn't *looked* at a man since, and none will look at her. Your Jammer did that."

"He's not *my* Jammer."

"Just keep your eyes open for him, Korrin. You're as good as a man can be in these times, and I like you. I'd hate to hear they found you butchered in the street."

Madone's words chilled me. I knew the kind of people who came through the brothel, and to pick someone out as being especially bad was quite something. *And why would Rhyl Santon employ such a man?* Another mystery. And that was my trade: mysteries. I took them and opened them up, coming in from left and right, before or after, and eventually I dissected them and presented them for view. Usually they revealed themselves without a fight. I had a feeling that this one would be different.

"Thank you for the warning," I said. "I look after myself."

"I know that," Madone said, and I was pleased to see her smile return.

Back in the hallway the tinkle of water covered the sighs, grunts and screams from around the building. The sheebok turned its circles, never arriving and never leaving, and soon it would die and be replaced by another. At least it was fed. It had a purpose. I put my hand through the false pocket and clasped the crossbow on my belt before heading for the door.

"Korrin?" Madone said. "Next time, just come for a fuck."

"I'm saving myself for you!" I called over my shoulder. I heard Madone's soft laugh at our usual exchange, and its familiarity made it all the more difficult going back onto the street.

Jammer was out there, waiting for me. He emerged from shadows and walked past me, away from the brothel and the memories of whatever terrible thing he had done in there. I watched the muscles flexing on his back, outlined beneath his jacket and shaded by poor lantern-light. I wondered how many people would miss him if I put a bolt into his spine.

"So where are we going now?" he asked without turning around. He was leading, yet he asked me the way. I found that to be a good omen.

"We're going to buy some wine," I said.

He grunted, paused to let me by, and I felt his gaze on my back as we headed toward the markets that lined the main route into the heart of Noreela City. ✧

4

I DRANK a lot of rotwine. Many people in Noreela did, because it was easily made from common fruits, cheap to buy and efficient at taking away reality for days at a time. It was called rotwine because of its effects on the body. But like fledge and gush ants, and the more exotic drugs from southern parts of Noreela, its obvious dangers did little to dissuade people from using it. These days rot was endemic, and few saw any point in trying to evade it.

I had tried more expensive wines a few times, usually at the behest of rich clients. I liked them—they were vivid and fruity, smooth and pleasing—but none had the gritty immediacy of rotwine. Drinking a rich person's wine was like tasting a future that could never be. There was something false about them, a hint at fake goodness when much was grey and dark. I felt uncomfortable drinking something like that, as though it would remove me from my own reality. I was a Bajuman, relatively poor and struggling to survive like everyone else in a world that supported us less and less. Rich people fought the same struggle, but they denied the truth by surrounding themselves with things perceived as "fine". Expensive wines did not protect them against the Great Plagues. Fresh fish imported from the Bay of Cantrassa did little to guard them against the taint of local crops. Clothes weaved in Long Marrakash did not deflect a thief's knife, and ignoring the rot could not make the future fresh.

So, rotwine was my choice. It was an honest drink, and I welcomed its mind-calming effects as much as anyone.

I paused on the way to the wine traders' market. It was still dark, and dawn was barely a smudge between the high buildings to the east.

"Why are we stopping?" Jammer asked behind me.

"Breakfast, Jammer," I said. I saw the look of anger as he turned away. He hated me using the name he had tried to keep a secret.

"I'm not hungry."

"Then watch me eat." I bought some grilled sheebok and fried potatoes from an early street trader, wrapped them in the thin sheet of bark they came on and waited for them to cool. "Shall we sit?" I walked through a narrow alley and emerged into a large square, bounded on all sides by three-storey buildings that housed courts and rooms for militia. There were already about twenty people sitting on stone benches around the square, eating an early breakfast or drinking a late bottle of rotwine. There were always people here at this hour, when the city hovered between the hidden dangers of night and the more visible troubles of daytime. I supposed they felt safe in this place where law pretended to rule. I came here purely to watch them, and learn, and sometimes to make another contact that could help me in the future.

"Why here?" Jammer asked, glancing up at the darkened windows.

"Afraid you'll see more of your old friends?" I looked down at the food parcel and smiled as I unwrapped my breakfast. *Mage-shit, if I keep on like this it'll be my fault when he finally crushes my head between those big hands.* Humour had always been my best defence, and taunting this mercenary made me smile. Perhaps I really was self-destructive.

"Just don't talk to me, Bajuman."

"Then stop asking me questions." I bit into the food and sighed as the heat coursed through my body. The meat was not fresh—it was heavy with salt, and beneath that I could taste the raw tang of decay—but the spiced oils masked most of the flavour, and the potatoes were excellent. I finished quickly, licked my fingers, rolled up the bark and crushed it into a pocket.

We remained sitting side by side, silent, on edge, as the sun lit the sky to the east and poured into the square.

"So why wine?" Jammer asked. Perhaps silence gave him too much time to think.

"A wine trader from the Northern Districts visited the brothel," I said. "He's procuring wine for a special dinner party. Forbidden foods."

Jammer nodded. "Find me the man and I can beat the truth from him."

I sat up straight, still having to look up into Jammer's eyes. "You're following me, not doing my job," I said. "Be a good mercenary and let me do things my way."

His mouth twisted into a growl and I saw rage simmering in his eyes. He leaned in closer, fingernails scraping across the stone bench as he fisted his hands.

This time, I was faster.

I had the knife pressed against Jammer's left side before he could raise his hands. I nudged it forward until I felt it pierce his clothing. His eyes widened when he felt the cool metal touch his skin, and he glanced around, looking left and right.

"Let's not do this," I said calmly.

He smiled. "As you wish, Bajuman."

"My name's—"

"Let's not do this. Yet." He reached down and pushed my hand away from his side, glancing down at the knife. "A militia blade. And well kept, too."

"Payment for a job," I said. "It's yet to taste blood."

Jammer stood and stretched to his full height, reaching skyward. I heard his joints click. "A knife that's unblooded is as useless as a cock that's unwetted," he said.

I shook my head and stood, sheathed the knife, walked away. Jammer followed me and I sensed the glow of his pride. I wondered which one of us was ahead.

WE ARRIVED at the Noreela City Wine Exchange in time to watch the traders setting their stalls. The Exchange was in a large covered enclosure, the roof supported by carved stone columns, windows colourful spreads of stained glass. Some illustrated images from Noreela's long history, but most had been broken and repaired so often that their stories were in shards. Dawn struck the windows and gave the Exchange floor a wonderful splash of colour. Birds fluttered beneath the high roof. Small shadows darted along at the base of the wall, disappearing into holes in the skirtings. I stood at the wide open entrance and stared inside, and the smell of spilled wine hung in the air, still fresh.

There were at least fifteen traders jostling for space. A fat, sweating man lumbered from one trader to the next, questioning them and writing in a small book. He tried to suggest where to set up their stalls, but the dealers made up their own minds. Several squabbles broke out, and the fat man's intervention only made matters worse. His clothes were soaked with sweat, his face glowed red, and I expected him to collapse at any moment.

"Order," he muttered as he crossed and re-crossed the Exchange floor. "There must be *order*!"

A bottle smashed and the scent of wine grew stronger. Somebody shouted, someone else was blamed, and the fat man stood in the centre and wiped his face with his sleeve.

I entered the Exchange, feeling the chill as I passed into the influence of the great building. Sunlight flooded through the tall windows, but they seemed to bleed its heat.

Jammer followed. His shadow surrounded me.

"We should be looking in the pits and dives, not places like this," he said.

"I'm the hunter. Let me hunt."

The first trader I approached was stocking a stepped table with bottles of amber fluid. I recognised the honey wine from Ventgoria, an expensive, exclusive bottle which would cost more than I made in a week.

"Not trading yet," the man said, glancing at me, staring at Jammer.

"I'm in a rush," I said. "You haven't put your price marks up yet, I see?"

The trader smiled. "Open to negotiation." His clipped words were normal in Ventgorians. The atmosphere in that place was often laden with toxins from the ground, and they had learned to keep their breathing fast and shallow.

"I'm having a dinner party," I said. "Very special party. Lots of important guests. And I'm looking for just the right wine to compliment the main course."

"Main course would be?"

I made a pretence of looking over my shoulder, casting furtive glances at the other traders. "Rare," I said.

The trader nodded. "Many rare meals, nowadays."

"Many?"

Jammer grasped my shoulder and pressed his face against my ear. His breath was warm and sickly. "We're looking down the wrong route."

I ignored him. "Many?" I asked again.

"Sold fifteen bottles yesterday. Same. Negotiable." The trader smiled again, and I realised that it did not suit his face.

Jammer let go and stepped back. His shadow left me, and I felt my shoulders relax.

"Can you tell me who?" I asked. I leaned in close and waved the trader toward me, including him in my secret. "Only, I wouldn't want to replicate someone else's menu. You know? Wouldn't look good at all." I fingered one of the bottles, ran my fingers around the bark stopper, smelled my finger. I sighed. "Delightful!"

"We don't need a name," Jammer said. He stood by my side and glared at the trader. "Just point him out."

"If he knows we've been asking—"

"Shut up, Bajuman!" He spat at my feet. I felt it hit the soft leather of my shoe. I also sensed the sudden change in the trader.

"Bajuman?"

"Of course he is," Jammer said. "Can't you smell the stink of it on him?"

The trader was smiling. "Good for you," he said. And then he looked over my shoulder and nodded at a man walking into the Exchange.

I turned, trying to appear casual, but Jammer was already upon him. I saw the man's eyes open wide in surprise, and then the mercenary's fist crushed his lips against his teeth. "A talk!" Jammer boomed, and he dragged the man from the Exchange.

"Thank you," I said to the Ventgorian trader, but the smile had fallen from his face, and his expression was now icy cold.

I hurried from the building, feeling the stares of two dozen men and women following me out. *How is this going so wrong?* I thought. But it was more than wrong. It was not only control I had lost to Jammer, it was knowledge. He now had me at a disadvantage, and I had no idea how to regain the initiative other than to leave him behind.

And that would not do. For all the interest I had in this case, I still needed the fee.

I followed the sounds of violence. Grunts and gasps, punches, mumbled words and vicious sneers. Jammer had taken the man around the side of the Exchange to beat him, and I found the mercenary dangling him over a ditch filled with broken bottles. If he fell in there the wine trader would survive, but crawling out would scar him for life.

"Don't drop him," I said. "We're here to ask him questions, not hurt him."

"I've asked, and he knows nothing. He's not working for our people."

"How can you be so sure?"

"You want to ask as well, Bajuman?" Jammer edged the man my way. His face was a bloody ruin, eyes glaring white from a mask of red. I could see the shrapnel of shattered teeth on his lips and chin.

"Why did you hit him?" I asked. "We could have—"

"Asked nicely? Fod Larima's time is short, if he isn't dead already. Have we really got time to be polite? Besides, everyone's guilty of something."

"Still no need to put him in the glass pit," I said.

Jammer tilted his head for a moment, considering. Then he dropped the man to the ground.

A group of people from the Exchange came to see what was happening. This man was obviously a valued client if the traders felt courageous enough to come to his aid.

"We should leave," I said. Jammer gave the man one final kick in the ribs and started on his way.

I went to follow, then knelt quickly by the man's side. "Do you know Jammer?" I asked. I thought he would answer, that given a friendly face and a calm tone of voice, I would coax some truths from him. But the man simply closed his eyes, his breathing coming shorter and faster. When someone approached behind me I hurried after Jammer. Last thing I wanted now was to be caught in a lynching. I had a feeling that the mercenary would do little to help.

———

"SO WHAT did you ask him?" We had passed through several narrow alleys and across an enclosed square, its fountain empty and dry since the Plague Laws had forbidden water ornamentation. I was certain that we were not being followed, yet I kept an ear open. Jammer seemed unconcerned.

"I asked him for a menu."

"And he told you just like that?"

"I'm persuasive."

I walked alongside the big man, thinking of the persuasion he may have used on the whore. I hoped he never had a question for me.

"How do you know he told the truth?"

"Because I know when people lie. When truth is so rare, it stands out."

"So where now?" I asked, knowing that the question would annoy him. Jammer stopped and looked back at me.

"Don't ask me, you're in the lead."

I walked past him, choosing a route that would take us back to the main street to the centre of Noreela City. A few beats later I heard the mercenary following close behind.

"More breakfast," I said. "Always a good place to start again."

AS I walked I thought over what Rhyl Santon had told me. Her friend, a fodder, had been stolen. She had come to me because I was a hunter, and she did not seem to mind that I was Bajuman. She wanted Fod Larima found before he was eaten. She could think of no other reason why he had been taken away; there had been no ransom demand. Jammer had battered the wine trader who may have been procuring wine for a special meal...perhaps a meal involving fodder...and now I was without a lead once more.

Still, Santon was paying me by the day. But Fod Larima probably didn't have many days left.

"You know he's dead already, don't you?" I said. I knew Jammer heard, though he did not answer. Someone sleeping beneath an old blanket in the narrow alley sat upright and shouted, laying back down when he saw Jammer's bulk. "Dead, cut up, eaten."

"He'd better not be," Jammer said.

"Stress doesn't improve the taste, so I'm told. Not that I'd ever try to eat one of the poor things. But then I also can't understand why people hate Bajumans so much."

"Because you're scum!" Jammer said.

We were nearing the end of the alley, and I could see people passing back and forth in the street ahead. Morning traders, others on their way to work, some perhaps on their way home. Whores and prophets, militia and doctors, a witch and a man who may have once been Shantasi.

"I bet you don't even know the story," I said. "You hate us because you're bred to hate us. By your parents, and theirs before them, and I'll bet none of them knew the truth."

"You're disease carriers," he said. "You polluted the Noreelan bloodline five hundred years ago, and the land is still trying to rid itself of your taint. If I had my way you'd all be buried alive."

I shook my head, knowing that I could never argue with such deep-rooted hostility. No Bajuman had ever hurt Jammer, nor his parents, nor anyone he cared for. No Bajuman had ever done anything against him. He did not understand, and he would never accept the truth.

I stopped and turned back to the big man. "I look the same as you," I said. "I speak the same, I—"

"But your blood stinks of shit," he said. He could barely even look at me.

I berated myself for even attempting to talk to this ignorant. "Believe whatever you have to," I said. "But Larima is already dead." I stepped out into the street and submitted myself to the ebb and flow of Noreela City.

WE CAME to Peak Dash Square, a huge place toward the centre of the city where it was easy to lose a day. There were shoppers and entertainers, beggars and militia, and around its edges the more affluent traders were opening their shops, lifting their awnings, carrying out their tables and displaying their wares. Fruit and meat, fish and leather goods, live animals and dead; the smells soon permeated the air. Food vendors had already set up in their usual circle at the centre of the huge space, and people were gravitating their way.

"What are we doing here?" Jammer said. I'd already seen him eyeing the few militia who milled around, looking to see whether he knew any of them. He seemed to relax a little, so I assumed he did not.

"Like I said, breakfast. Poached fish, I think. They'll say it's from the Western Shores. I'll say, like Mage-shit it is. Then we'll haggle, and I'll buy, and you and I will sit to—"

"I don't sit at table with Bajuman," Jammer said.

I shrugged and walked on. A gaggle of old women passed me by, and I noticed that all but one were blinded by cataracts. One of the less damaging of the Great Plagues, still the blinding had left thousands without sight. I suspected that the one woman who could still see was lining her pockets with these poor victims' money.

I reached the food stalls and walked slowly around the full circle, examining their produce and taking even greater note of the cooking methods. Many traders failed to wash their skillets and hotplates from one day to the next, and I had no wish to be laid up vomiting and shitting like a sheebok. There was a huge variety of food on display, but I did as I'd already suggested to Jammer and went for the fish.

"Fresh from the Western Shores!" the woman behind the stall said, and I smiled and shook my head.

Fish procured, I sat at a small round table, rested my feet on the wooden chair beside me and began to eat. Jammer hovering at the periphery of my vision was distracting, and I could not get comfortable. I looked at him but he glanced away.

Later, he came to sit down. He'd bought a tray of fried spiced meats and mashed tate, and he ate without looking at me.

"Which trader did you buy that from?" I asked.

He did not reply. He ate in a very mannered way, I noticed, keeping his mouth closed and not spilling a drop. It didn't suit his image.

"Not that foul-talking meat mutt from the Cantrass Plains?"

He glanced at me, chewed, looked away and wiped at the corner of his mouth.

I shook my head and sighed. "He never cleans his knives. Half of what you're eating is two days old."

Jammer continued chewing but his posture had changed. He refused to stop eating at the behest of a Bajuman, but he was no longer enjoying his meal.

I smiled, relaxed back in my chair and watched the world go by.

"THIS IS useless," Jammer said. "You hear me, Bajuman? You asleep? This is useless!"

I lifted my head, looked around, and rested my chin on my chest once more. "Quiet," I said. "I'm working."

"Working?" Jammer stood and sent his chair tumbling backward.

I cursed. An hour, perhaps a little more, and my opportunity for contemplation was over. I often did my best work with my eyes closed and my mind in free spin, random thoughts colliding, repulsing or coalescing into larger truths comprised of the small whispers I already knew. This case was still young, but already there were shadows and allusions. Sometimes, what I didn't know told me more that what I did.

Of one thing I was certain: Jammer was more than my shadow. He was *involved.*

"More food?" I asked.

Jammer shook his head and looked away, exasperated. Good. This time, he would not follow.

"I need more food. Feeds my brain."

"Makes you fat."

"Fat with knowledge." I stood and walked casually towards the circle of vendors. I sensed Jammer watching me, could almost hear the hesitation that tensed his leg muscles and eased them again. If he followed then I would have to eat again. If he did not...perhaps I could question someone without him smashing their face to pulp.

I reached the stalls and walked slowly around the circle, browsing and asking a few questions before moving on. A few people nudged into me and apologised, while the majority recognised me as a Bajuman and steered away. Neither bothered me too much. Their ignorance or recognition made me a part of the crowd, and that was fine.

Before one stall selling pickled wellburr leaves hung several large polished plates. I paused, located myself in the reflection and looked farther. Jammer was still sitting down, resting with his elbows on his knees and staring down at the ground.

I moved quickly until the circle of stalls hid me from sight, then hurried across to the corner of the square.

An old acquaintance of mine owned a shop there selling truffles. And what exclusive dinner party would be complete without the fruit of the land?

"KORRIN! YOU streak of sheebok shit, why have you been avoiding me?"

"Can't afford truffles."

Rofold Bigg smiled and showed me his black gums. He took pride in them. He never smiled at real customers—their trade was too "mannered", so he said—and he thought hiding his rotten mouth from them put him at some sort of advantage. I had never figured out why, and never thought to ask. Each to their own.

Rofold waved me in. "Come in, shut the door! Business is slow lately, I'm sure we won't be disturbed. Rotwine?"

I shook my head. Years ago Rofold and I had spent two days on a rotwine binge, paid for with the gains from a particularly fruitful case that he'd helped me solve. Soon after that the Plagues hit, and we had been out of touch ever since. "No time," I said. "I'm in a rush. Glad to see you didn't die in the Plagues."

"Someone told me you had."

"Still here."

He gestured at his shop, and the fungi nestling in their soft leather baskets. "And so am I!"

"Business is slow?"

Rofold's smile slipped, but only a little. "I guessed you hadn't come just to stay in touch."

I shrugged. "I apologise." I browsed the warty produce.

"Yes, business is slow."

"Dipping your fingers into any other exotic food markets?"

Rofold's smile had almost vanished. I felt guilty at that—he'd seemed genuinely pleased to see me—but the back of my neck was already starting to itch. *He's probably looking for me already*, I thought.

"What do you think I am, Korrin?"

"I know what you are, Rofold. A businessman trying to make a living. I'm not accusing you, simply enquiring."

Rofold was businesslike once again, and he knew what I dealt in. "Information," he said. "If I have some, you will pay for it."

"Fair enough."

"So, what sort of exotic food?"

"Very exotic. Forbidden."

His eyes narrowed, and I knew that he knew. I turned away and examined the truffles. I needed to keep his price down to a level I could afford.

"Why are you in such a rush?"

"Someone's following me."

"And you led them here?"

Not sure yet, I thought. "They're not dangerous to you." My first real lie of the day.

"So how much are you willing to pay to get what you want and leave quickly?"

I looked directly at Rofold, remembering our drunken days together. "Twenty tellans for a friend."

Rofold's stern expression held for a few beats, but then he smiled again. I was happy to see those black gums. "A friend?"

I nodded.

"Then a friend is worth twenty-five, surely?"

"Of course." As I plucked a coin purse from my pocket, Rofold told me about the fodder.

"I've heard he was taken, and those that took him went down into Copeland."

I paused as I handed over the coins. "Why?"

Rofold shrugged. "How should I know? Maybe Cope is planning a feast."

"Even Cope would never eat fodder."

"How does anyone know what that mad dog would do? Maybe he's making friends. Or maybe he'll sell him on."

I dropped the coins in Rofold's hands and he hid them away beneath his counter. "It doesn't make sense."

And it made things much more difficult. Copeland was not a good place to be, even for a Bajuman. Though I knew a few of the ways in, I had never been there because I valued my existence.

But now, if I had to go, it would need to be without Jammer. Ex-militia he may be, but down there if we were seen together, we'd die together.

Copeland, I thought. *Shit*.

"Your friend?" Rofold said, staring over my shoulder.

I turned around and Jammer was standing at the open door, blocking most of the light from outside. I heard Rofold slink away to the rear of his shop leaving me, the mercenary and the truffles.

He was panting. He'd been running. Now I knew it was my turn.

"Trying to give me the—"

I pulled a knife and sliced my palm. It hurt, and I shouted, and that distracted Jammer long enough for me to flick my blood his way.

His eyes went wide as he tried to fall back. I was already running, shaking my hand, spraying bloody droplets into the air at the big man. And even if deep down he knew that the stories about the Bajuman were exaggerated, still he was on the ground by the time I leapt over his splayed legs, hands over his nose and mouth, desperate to avoid inhaling any of my filth.

Although I was already past him, I paused long enough to flick another slick of blood at his wide, terrified eyes.

Then I ran. Ducked into the crowd, slipped left and right, skirted around the food vendors before darting into a leather shop, leaping the counter and shrugging off its angry owner's hands as I sought the rear entrance.

He would follow. But if I took advantage of my lead, I would be descending into Copeland before Jammer knew where I had gone.

Sorry, Rofold, I thought. Jammer would go back and question him when he realised he'd lost me. I only hoped that Rofold would not pretend to be brave. ⌒

5

COPELAND: DIRTY, deep, lawless and dark, home to
criminals and runaways and those that can't decide which
they are. Some called it a city underground, others called it
the city's underground. Many dared not name it, because to
talk of Copeland was to be aware of it, and awareness pro-
moted thought, and to dwell on somewhere so dangerous
meant you would not get to sleep at night. Copeland, the
place in Noreela City where anything was possible, and death
and pain were probable. There were barriers even there, lines
that should not be crossed, but they were drawn by Cope
or—if the rumours of his death during the Great Plagues
were to be believed—his descendants. Copeland was his
place, and whether he was still alive or mouldering in his
grave it always would be. His history hung like a constant
breath in those subterranean passages and caves, those underground squares and bottomless pits. His story was so large
that he existed above ground as well, throbbing through
the dark underbelly of the city like its diseased twin heart.
Some said Cope had Violet Dog blood in him, but the Violet
Dogs themselves were little more than myth. Some said that
when he spoke in the dark his eyes shone red, but I'd never
met anyone who had actually *seen* that. Like all good myths
it was built on accounts handed down a dozen times, and

made all the more stronger because of that. Cope was such a terrifying entity that people did not dare disbelieve. They had faith in his awfulness.

Copeland: through all my years in Noreela City, and all the cases, I'd never had cause to go down there. I'd once known another hunter who descended looking for a lost man, and came back half a man himself. They'd taken his legs and genitals, then drugged him so he could live through the agony of healing. One of the plagues got him in the end. But it was Copeland that killed him.

Copeland: the end of the line, perhaps. Or the start of a new one. Either way, I was afraid. Bajuman I may be, but being shunned by most was no ticket into Copeland. To be accepted down there could never be so simple.

IT WAS gone midday, so I made my way through the streets toward the Arch of Kaldas. This ancient building had been here when Noreela City was young, built by an unknown tribe as an offering to forgotten gods. It was surrounded by cracked pedestals, from which the statues had long since fallen away. Some took interest in the place, but it was haunted, so not many people came here anymore. I guessed the haunting was a convenient story to keep people away, but I never had cause to find out until now.

I had known for a long time that this was one way into Copeland.

Copeland had several entrances and dozens of exits. The entrances could be survived, with care. Most of the exits were for dead people. The Arch of Kaldas had been used before; I had spoken to people who went in and came out this way, and one of them had given me the key. For a price, of course. Everything in Noreela City had a price. I was about to claim a return on my investment.

As the sun reached its zenith I emerged into the open area around the Arch. The ground here was rocky and untouched for generations, sprouting the smashed pedestals here and there, weeds bearing startling purple flowers growing from cracks in the stone. I wondered why no one had tried picking the flowers to smoke or sell, but the haunting tale had spread far and wide. It was never dwelled upon too much— the Arch was an old building with little use, so no one really cared. But it was said that these ghosts would kill.

I waited for a while beside one of the ruined pedestals, wondering which god had once stood upon this base. I checked my crossbow. My knife was still bloody and I left it that way. The short sword on my belt felt heavier now that I was more aware of its presence. I hoped that I would not have to use it.

I was impatient to go but aware that I needed to wait. Jammer would be following me. He had no idea which direction I had taken, but still the hairs on my neck stood straight and my balls tingled. I had used his own weaknesses to better him this time, but I knew that in a stand up fight, he would always win. An abuser of whores he may be, but he was also a mercenary and ex-militia. Someone like Rhyl Santon would not hire a man like him unless she knew he could fight.

Something shifted across the dusty ground alongside the wall of the Arch. I held my breath and grew still, turning my eyes to look because I dared not turn my head. Any slight movement would give me away. My heart hammered, and I craved another mouthful of rush ants. After this was over, I promised myself, I would indulge.

Nothing moved. Perhaps it had been a breeze.

It was almost time. I had calculated the time of year and the angle of the sun, and I hoped I was right. I could see the main entrance of the Arch of Kaldas from here—a square, hollow building rather than the arch its name implied—and the sun was casting the shadow that should guide me in. I felt a thrill using such arcane wisdom.

I moved from one pedestal to another, trying to avoid the stark sunlight, and as I stepped into the shadow of the Arch I heard movement. It came from very close by, a whisper of cloth against stone, but I could see no one.

"Who's there?" I said, cringing at my own stupidity.

The sound came closer, though I could not tell whether it was in front of me, or behind. I moved toward the entrance to the Arch, eager not to miss the appointed time. If it passed by then so would my chance to enter Copeland, for today at least.

The noise moved ahead of me, and also followed.

As I stepped into the Arch the noise ceased. Did it know me? Had it seen inside? I probed inward but sensed no intrusion, and when I extended my senses outward I was alone once more. I was sweating and panting, but also elated. Something indefinably strange had just happened, yet I had never once felt in danger.

I took out my knife and knelt in the sun streaming into the entrance. I traced the blade where sunlight met shadow cast by the Arch, and it cut a finger's length into the stone. I paused, cut along the shadow in a different direction, and then rock grumbled as a triangle of ground fell away before me. Beyond it, below, the faint illumination of hidden depths.

Glancing around, sheathing my knife but keeping hold of the small crossbow, I stepped into the hole. I hoped that I was not saying goodbye to Noreela City forever.

I WENT down. The tunnel was rough and dangerous, flat one moment, dipping steeply around a corner the next. It was designed for someone to know, I realised, not for casual visitors like myself. This was not a place that welcomed occasional guests.

I wondered whether Fod Larima had been dragged this way.

The illumination I had seen came from somewhere farther down. I could just make out the floor before me, the rugged walls still displaying marks from the tools used to forge the tunnel, and here and there writing in a language I did not understand. Some of the lettering was familiar, but the words made no sense. I wondered what they said, and I felt an awful sense of exclusion.

Smells came up to me; cooking, sweat, other odours I could not identify.

They said that Copeland was massive, having branches, tunnels and caves beneath much of Noreela City. Many of these were merely passageways from one place to another, but there were dozens of centres of habitation down here. Usually the inhabitants lived in peace with each other, but there were tales of subterranean battles overseen by Cope himself. It was a whole new world.

I went on, working through a brief rush of claustrophobia. This was not a place to panic.

And I suddenly wondered what I was doing down here. I was a Bajuman hunter, nothing more. What could I hope to gain by descending into this forbidden world? Punishment for knowing the method of entry, perhaps. Pain, just for being here. Maybe they would kill me and cut me up, feed me out of one of the many exits for dead people, leave my parts to be discovered on some remote street or in the corner of a rarely frequented square. How could I possibly hope to come down here and begin asking questions?

I paused. It was still utterly silent. The tunnel turned a few steps ahead, heading left and down. Each corner took me closer, and each step closer placed me more in danger.

As I turned to leave, something came at me.

It roared, I screamed. It bore down on me, spinning around the corner and along the tunnel, knocking me from my feet, straddling my chest, pressing itself down so that I had no hope of drawing the crossbow. Its jaws slavered above my head, saliva dripping onto my face.

I struggled and kicked out, hot with panic. I could not move my arms. The hound sniffed at me and growled again.

"Back!" a woman's voice said. The hound withdrew, raking its nails down my chest as a parting gesture.

I went to sit up and a sword pressed under my chin. "Not so fast, Bajuman."

All I could see was her silhouette. She was small, thin, her hair forming a wild halo against the subdued light. "I'm no harm," I said.

She laughed. "How right you are!" She sniffed and wiped her sleeve across her face. "So, what's your business down here? Want to commit suicide?"

"I'm looking for someone," I said. "A friend."

"What's his name?"

"It's a her." I don't know why I lied. Perhaps because I felt some need to maintain control, not give everything away.

"So...what's *her* name then, Bajuman?"

"I tell you, you know her, you might just kill me."

"Depending on my curiosity to save your skin?"

"Perhaps." I squinted, trying to see the woman better. For some reason she obliged, stepping sideways so that light from below lit her face. The hound sat patiently by her feet as she smiled down at me.

"Bajuman," I said.

"So?"

"So nothing. I just don't meet many of us."

"Us?" She spat at my feet, pressed the sword forward again. "You're as bad as *them*, talking about *us* as if we're different."

"We are," I say.

"How?" The word was like a punch, a challenge, an offer of violence. I felt the tip of the sword break my skin, aching to go deeper.

"We're better than them," I said. "That's all. That's how we're different."

She paused, head cocked to one side. "You believe that?"

"I know that. What's your name?"

"None of your mage-shitting business." But she stood back and removed the sword, and I knew that I would survive this first meeting at least.

The woman and her hound turned suddenly and started back along the tunnel. "This way," she said. "You must really want to find this woman to come down here after her."

"I do," I say.

She looked back over her shoulder. "Not much chance if you won't tell her name."

"My mage-shitting business," I said. She didn't smile, but kept on walking.

I uttered a shaky sigh and touched the bloody smear beneath my chin.

"IS COPE still alive?" I asked. "Is he down here now? Is he really descended from a Violet Dog?" Perhaps I was filled with too much bravado after surviving that first encounter, but I felt safe asking such questions.

The woman also felt safe not responding. I wondered whether she really wanted me to follow her. Was she leading me somewhere, or simply using the same tunnel as me? We came to several junctions, and I always took the same branch as her, but she and her hound never looked back.

The illumination came from cave mites. There were nests of them at frequent intervals, great crawling, rolling gatherings that produced their own heat and light to warm the eggs at their centres. The shapes of their nests seemed to change, offering a bulge that tracked me as I passed by. I could not shake the idea that they were watching me go.

"We're here," the woman said at last. And we were. We stepped from the tunnel into a larger place, and the sight winded me.

I had never suspected that it would be anything like this. ⌒

6

I HAD seen many old machines, parts of machines, and scraps of metal and stone that were once machines, but which now were damaged and mutilated beyond recognition. There were everywhere in Noreela City. They were incorporated into buildings, for structure or obscure aesthetics. Their solid skins paved roads and footpaths. In some of the parks they stood almost as statues to history, strange memoirs of a time gone by. For all the good they apparently brought the land in the past, they were somewhat derided now, although it was a derision that grew from fear. They had once moved—had, so some said, been alive—and now they were still and dead. That scared many people. Looking at an old, decaying machine was like staring at the side of a cliff and thinking, *That once had a mind.* Unfathomable, unbelievable. Perhaps they had breathed. Maybe, in those final terrible days, they had bled.

The cavern I stared into was formed from a complete machine. I had never heard of or imagined anything so large, not even in dreams. It was staggering. Its spherical shell formed the walls, rising around me and closing in high overhead, meeting at a point where a bolt thicker that three men held the whole place together.

"The fuck bolt," the woman said. She seemed to be enjoying my astonishment. She was smiling.

"Because it's shaped…?" I could not finish my sentence, and her smile broadened.

"Last thing we'd all say if it fell. I have to leave you. Good hunting." And before I could say more the woman and her hound moved quickly away, climbing a metal slatted staircase and disappearing into a warren of nest-like rooms above my head.

I could barely move. I stood there taking everything in, and if I had ever intended trying to blend into the surroundings, my plan was already a failure. My mouth hung open as if to say, *Yes, I'm new here.*

Much of the interior of the machine was still here, solidified and petrified, and put to use by the new inhabitants of this place. I could not help thinking of them as parasites, making a home inside this once moving thing. There were bridges formed from smooth stone, hollow rooms suspended from walls and ceiling by thick bracings that shone like metal, and the walls of the sphere were pocked with holes and rough doorways. Whether these had been a part of the original machine, I could not tell. Perhaps they had been breathing ports or holes for other, more enigmatic means. Or maybe these underground dwellers had cut them there themselves.

I could see a hundred people moving at any one time. Their movements were illuminated by flaming torches and oil lanterns tied to walls, hung from the dozens of struts that spanned from one side to the other, or suspended in metal baskets from the ceiling high above. The fuck bolt was festooned with a score of huge, burning baskets, fuelled by oil pumped in through pipes that snaked around the walls like petrified veins.

And the noise was tremendous. People talking, laughing or arguing. The hiss of steam-cooking. The clang of metallic tools. The shuffling of feet, the regular impact of construction or destruction, and from somewhere close by the grunts of someone rutting. So much life inside this dead thing, though all of it dangerous.

What could this machine's purpose have been? A tunnel digger, perhaps? But for what? Or maybe it had existed on the surface, enacting some mysterious purpose before the Cataclysmic War drove it underground to die. Whatever its history, it sent a chill through me to think of what it had been, and what it had become.

I started walking, afraid that if I stood still for too long I would attract unwanted attention. There was a wide path circling the cavern at this level, with rough stone stair-cases leading down and rope ladders, strutted poles or metal stairs leading up. A man lowered himself down close to me, glanced my way and then disappeared into a hole in the walkway.

Fod Larima, I thought. *He's why I'm here. Find him and leave, Korrin. There's nothing here for you.*

"Nothing here for you," a voice said, and for a second I thought I had spoken it myself. I looked for the source of the voice, and the sight of the face leering at me from above made me dizzy. I closed my eyes and felt the ground shift, and for a beat I thought the machine itself was moving. Then I realised it was my own head put in a spin. *He's hanging upside down*, I thought. I looked again at the inverted man. His face was bright red, his hair long and dropping almost to the walkway. His grin was a sad, down-turned mouth.

"Careful!" the man said, setting himself swinging left to right. But my initial wooziness had passed.

"Looking for someone," I said. "Help me find him, I'll pay you well."

"Well?" the man said. "What's well?" His voice seemed distorted by his unusual attitude. I wondered how long he'd been hanging like this. I glanced up at his feet, but they were out of sight in the leathery underside of one of the suspended rooms.

"Five tellans."

"Kill him?"

"Who?"

"When you find him, this lost man, this mystery who's a stranger to you. You find him, you kill him?"

"No," I said. "And he's no stranger." I thought this point was important. For some reason, claiming to know the fodder seemed sensible.

"No?" the man said, as if perplexed. "Then why look for him?"

"To take him out."

"Out? Down there?" He jutted his chin up at the ceiling. "Doubt he wants to go."

"Oh, I think he does," I said. "I know Larima well. He was *brought* down here, he didn't come. This is no place for him."

"So let him help himself, this fodder."

"I didn't tell you he was fodder."

"With a name like Larima…."

"No," I said. And then I let silence fall. Challenged, I expected this upside-down man to crumple, or flee. He did neither. He fell.

He struck the polished stone walkway, grunted, rolled onto his side. "Who?" he shouted, looking up at where his feet had been held. "Who tries to kill me?" He was screeching now, struggling to stand on his head, arms and legs flailing at the air in a poor attempt at maintaining balance.

But there was no balance for him. His red face grew redder, and when I rolled him onto his back he was starting to spit and curse.

I looked around, afraid that his screams would draw attention but quickly realising I need not be concerned. Nobody was even looking our way. This was Copeland, and events such as this must be routine.

Then I glanced up at the rough hole where his feet had been held. There were rusted metal hooks there, and several leather straps shredded by fresh cuts. Nothing moved inside the room beyond the hole. But I felt watched.

I pressed my short knife hard against the fallen man's throat. "Bajuman blood on this blade," I said. "You want me to open you to it?"

He paused in his struggles, and for the first time I got a good look at his face from the right way up. It was distorted. His cheeks had flowed upward to almost cover his eyes, his top lip was raised to expose his teeth, and his chin was flat, the skin pressed close around his jawbone. He must have been hanging upside down for a very long time.

"Open me up then, murderer," he said. "I'm afraid of no Bajuman."

"I don't want to kill you. Just tell me what you know of Fod Larima."

"*Everyone* knows. He's famous down here. We're all pleased to have him." He began to giggle, a wretched, choking sound drawn from deep in his throat.

"Cope? Is *he* pleased, that mad Dog?"

The man whispered, "You cannot speak of Cope, or he will hear."

"He's still alive then?"

"I didn't say that."

"*Where is Fod Larima?*"

"Safe from the likes of you."

"You tell me, or by the Black I'll kill you here and now."

Something in my voice gave the man pause. He stopped struggling, submitted to his unexpected inversion and stared me in the eye. "You here to help him, or eat him?" he said.

"That's nothing to you." I pressed harder, sliding the knife against the man's throat, and could not help grimacing at the sight of his skin parting. The man froze, distorted eyes going wide. "That's a taster," I said. "Just broke the skin. Next time I push as well as slice. Ten beats and I'll be leaving footprints in your blood as I leave."

For a few moments I thought he was going to remain silent, and I would be faced with a stark decision; follow through on my threat and kill him, or let him rise, and lose any advantage I had gained.

"I know," he said. "I'll tell you. But please help me back up."

I helped. He was sick as I dragged a metal basket over to stand on, he moaned as I did my best to tie and fix the leather straps, and by the time I'd finished I thought perhaps he was dead. But when I asked if he was ready he leapt onto the basket, jumped at the straps and lifted himself, twisting the leather into knots and sighing as he let himself hang down once again. He stretched out his arms and waved at the air, luxuriating in his position.

"So?" I asked.

"Come close," he said. I did so, cautious but eager to hear. "The Red Tunnel," he whispered. "It's not long, but it's dangerous. Not many of us go down there...but that's where he's kept. You'll smell it before you see its colour. Over there, somewhere." He nodded at the far wall of the cavernous machine and then closed his eyes, as though falling asleep.

I took one last look up at his strapped feet, wondering again who had cut the leather and why. No Bajuman liked the feeling of being watched.

———

THE SMELL of the Red Tunnel reached me long before I saw its crimson glow. It was the stink of human waste, rotting meat, and a bastardised tang of Shantasi spice. It smelled of food and death and decay, and it matched the sickly hue. I stood before the tunnel, ignoring a question thrown at me by a passerby, and it looked like a wound in the world.

"Hey, Bajuman," the person said again. "I asked, are you running away or toward?"

I glanced at the short, stocky miner standing before me. His skin was dark, his eyes fierce white pits reflecting a thousand lights. He looked as though he could break my back with a flick of his wrist.

"Why do you ask?" I said. I did not want to show any weakness.

"Mercenary just came in looking for you," he said.

Jammer!

I nodded, displaying none of my surprise or dismay.

Jammer found his way in!

"Thanks," I said.

The miner nodded and walked away. What was that? Some sort of skewed code of honour? Or just a scheme to draw me and Jammer into a fight? I watched the miner retreat across a shaky rope and timber bridge, and then I looked around the interior of the vast machine again. The mercenary could be anywhere, watching me or slinking toward me along walkways, down ladders, up ropes. So be it. If an ex-militia could survive coming down here, then perhaps he really could be of use.

I had a sense of things coming to a close. A gut feeling. And I had learned to trust those implicitly.

TO BEGIN with, the tunnel was cold and bare and uninhabited. Once the smells and sounds of the cavern faded behind me the tunnel shrank quickly, narrowing until I could touch both walls with my outstretched hands, and just tall enough so that my head did not scrape the ceiling. The walls bore the scars of hand-held tools, and the carved signatures of those who had wielded them. And the stone shone red. I had never seen that before, nor heard of it. It gave no heat. The light was soft and diffuse and cast no shadow, but it was enough to light my way.

I paused now and then to look back. I still had that sense of being followed and watched, but there was no sign of pursuit. I could have run back the way I had come, I supposed, crossbow drawn ready to challenge the watcher. But that would have been bringing trouble closer and sooner. So I walked on, following the slowly undulating and twisting tunnel, quickly becoming comfortable in its level red light.

Coming to a close, I thought. *All of this will be over soon. A quick case, but with the fodder involved there was no other way. And really, he's probably already dead. They'll show me a pile of bones and his uneaten feet, and that's all I'll have to take back to show Rhyl Santon. His feet. Uneaten, because they step in shit. Hardly a suitable reminder of a friend's life.*

There was a sound behind me, the musical clang of metal against stone. A badly-wielded weapon? I paused for a beat to make sure I wasn't being rushed, then moved quickly on.

I came across the first dwelling. It was excavated into the tunnel wall, a hollow in the rock where someone had once lived. There was little sign of current habitation; a few scattered clothes, a shredded blanket, some crushed metal cooking pans. And in the back of the hollow, what looked like a crumpled skeleton. In this light the bare bones still looked bloody.

I hurried on, unsettled. However that person had been killed, their body had been left where it fell. Perhaps there was not even a scrap of society down here, but I still assumed they'd dispose of their dead.

As I moved deeper I found other hollows in the tunnel walls, and not all of them were empty. There were people down here, scared, feral, blood-red people who offered me the points of swords or the business ends of crossbows as I passed. None of them took me on. Perhaps I looked too strong; these people were weak and bedraggled. I wondered why they would choose to live down here. But then I saw the redness in one woman's eyes, realised that it was not only reflection, and I began to wonder at the quality of this light.

They seemed starved and wretched, but happy. Some of them smiled through toothless mouths. Their lips were cracked and bleeding, their knuckles raw around weapon handles, but their eyes were alight. More than anyone, I knew the signs of addiction.

I went on, passing more people and deeper caves. I wondered just how far down it went and how long it had taken to dig. Perhaps some of these people had been born down here. Surely most of them would die without seeing the

143

light. And with that thought, the walls and ceiling closed in and began to crush me down.

I began to pant, my heart racing, skin slick with the sweat of fear, when I turned a corner and saw a fodder standing in the tunnel before me.

His eyes went wide as he glanced down at my crossbow.

I shook my head, trying to communicate that I meant no harm.

Footsteps sounded behind me.

A man and woman rushed out from a curtained cave in the tunnel wall just beyond where the fodder stood. Their eyes were wide and bright, not yet stained red by the air of this place, and the man reached for a short sword strapped to his hip. "You," he growled, and his voice was venom.

I'd never seen him before, and I could not understand what he meant. But then I realised that he was not talking to me.

I span around just in time to be shoved aside by Jammer. I fell awkwardly into the tunnel floor, crossbow hand trapped beneath my body.

"*You!*" the man said again, shouting this time.

Fod Larima howled, a lonesome, desolate sound.

The man stepped forward, sword raised.

Jammer pulled a crossbow and shot him in the face. His other hand flicked out and a throwing star struck the woman in the eye, spike going deep. She whined and twitched as she fell to the ground.

Then the mercenary turned on me. ✺

7

IT SEEMED that I was down there forever. At first, upon waking from the dreadful beating dealt me by Jammer, all I could do was crawl. My one good eye—the other was swollen shut—saw red everywhere. That red light glowed from the walls and drew me closer to the rock. And close though I was, my nose dipped down many times during that crawl, touching the cool floor of the tunnel as though keen to penetrate and become stone myself. It was a bizarre feeling. Most of the time the floor only appeared bloody, but once or twice I dragged myself through wetness that made that image true.

I found a depression in the tunnel wall. It was barely large enough to lie in, but I felt more protected there. Rock, closer around me. Bleeding red.

I thought perhaps I woke a few times, but they were more likely periods of lesser unconsciousness. People came to talk to me, telling me things I should never know, and one of them reached out with a dagger made of cloudy crystal and slashed my throat ear to ear. I gagged and laughed as my blood added itself to the atmosphere of Copeland. When I woke my hand went to my neck, and I felt no relief when I found the skin there whole and undamaged.

More dreams, more visits that were probably unreal, and at last I awoke properly, alone and warm and smiling. I could feel the expression stretch my mouth, mimicking the slash in my throat that never was. I felt as though I *should* be happy, I *must* be happy, whether I liked it or not.

Later, I discovered I'd only been down there for two days. Maybe that's how I found it just possible to climb back out.

I passed through the hollow heart of that giant machine, receiving a few curious glances but little more. I was battered, bruised and bloodied from Jammer's beating. Some of my ribs were broken. I had little memory of the assault; I do recall trying to fight back, but I had been fooling myself all along. He was a big man, and a professional killer. As I ascended out of Copeland, I realised that he had meant for me to live.

I found a tunnel that led up, and climbed for what felt like days. The darkness skewed time, as did the sudden withdrawal from that strange red light. The tunnel turned, steps appeared here and there, and I passed by junctions with barely a pause. I didn't care. I was going forward and up, only because there was nothing to wait for, and at the time I did not care whether I made it out. I don't know why. I'm a Bajuman and we're strong, never defeatist. We take what the world throws at us and fight it. They say our blood is a poison in Noreela's bloodline, and only we can prove them wrong.

But I did find my way out, emerging from a street-level drain somewhere in the Eastern Districts. A few people paused to watch as I climbed from the ground and into the heat of a Noreelan day. None came to help.

———

I SHOULD have gone home, but Rhyl Santon owed me money. And more than that, she owed me an explanation.

Why send Jammer with me if his final order was to beat me half to death? Or had that been a quirk of his, and his alone? Call it pride, curiosity or fear, but I needed to know.

I went into the Northern Districts and caused something of a stir. Here lived people with money and power, and those who could pay for a semblance of calm and order. Several militia moved to stop me as I walked through the streets, but they saw something that gave them pause. I never knew what. I like to think it was the determination evident on my face, but I fear that in truth it was the sight of so much Bajuman blood. For most of that day, as dried blood coated my skin, hair and the inside of my clothes, I was somebody else's problem.

I used my hunter skills to find Santon's home; a question here, an overheard comment there. By the time the sun was sinking and spreading its red glare across the rooftops, I knew where my employer lived.

I watched for a while. I'd managed to steal some meat from outside a butcher's shop, and I sat in a statue's shadow in a small square, eating and staring at the heavy metal gates. Behind them were Rhyl Santon and the money she owed me. Behind them also, answers. And if those answers were bad, I would very likely never leave here alive.

"YOU LOOK terrible," Rhyl Santon said. She seemed genuinely concerned. She was bathing my wounds with her own hands, tying strips of binding cloth to keep the herb mixes tight against the worst cuts. She flexed her fingers and felt along my ribs, staring over my shoulder and frowning in concentration. "Two broken," she said.

"Your mercenary did this."

"Jammer?" she asked, shocked. Either she was an excellent actress, or Jammer had taken things his own way.

"After I found Fod Larima he ambushed us and killed the ones that took him. Fair enough. But then he turned on me."

Rhyl shook her head, touching a finger to her chin. *There, I thought. That's the first sign that she's lying. She looks too confused. She's hiding what she knows, not considering what she does not know.*

"He said you told him to kill me," I said.

"No!"

"Really? I've grown to quite like him. I think we developed something of a rapport, the two of us. I think he left me beaten half to death, thinking he'd fulfilled half of his task."

"Korrin, that is not true. Why would I have ordered something so...*vile?*"

"You don't look well, Rhyl."

She shook her head. "I drank too much last night. We had company."

"Celebrating Fod's release?"

Her eyes flickered, just for a beat. She couldn't stare right at me. *And there, I thought. More lies. More confusion.*

"Of course," she said. "We're delighted to have him home."

"How is he?"

"Happy. Resting. Really Korrin, I can't imagine why Jammer did such a thing. He's very loyal to me, and—"

"You must pay him well. You know he mutilates whores?"

Rhyl looked at me then, long and hard. Her eyes changed from concerned and confused, to something else. Something that told me she was totally, utterly in control and always had been. It scared me, and I reached for my short sword.

She smiled. "Really, Korrin, there's no need for that."

I sensed a movement behind me and there was Jammer, standing in a doorway. He barely even looked at me.

"How much do I owe you?" she asked.

"So you pay me and let me go?"

She looked genuinely taken aback. "Of course! What else were you expecting?"

Just murder, I thought. *That's all.*

I told her what she owed, and she paid me double. "For the problems you encountered," she said, without looking at her soldier-for-hire. "I'd like to thank you. It's so good to have Fod back among friends. He'd thank you himself, but he's a little shaken and—"

"And resting," I said.

"Yes, he's resting." Rhyl smiled again, but any warmth had vanished.

"Well, I believe I'll spend some time resting too," I said. "Glad to be of service."

"Jammer will see you out." She turned, left the room, and I never saw her again.

"After you," I said to the big mercenary. He smiled, and it was a genuine smirk. He let me follow him, exposing his back to my sword hand, but his gait was easy and relaxed. Not the walk of a man about to commit murder.

"How did you find your way own into Copeland?" I asked.

"I know Cope."

"Liar." He shrugged but did not turn around. *He can't,* I thought. *Even if Cope's still alive, this man is nothing to him. Is he?*

"Who are you?" I asked.

Jammer did stop then, leaning against a heavy timber door frame and crossing his arms. "If only you knew," he said. "Fucking Bajuman." He nodded at the door. "In there, out to the yard and through the back entrance. And if I ever see you again, I'll kill you for real." And still he smiled, sharing a joke with himself. As he walked away I heard a snort of derision.

I walked into the large kitchen, and I suppose somewhere deep down I already knew what I was going to find. The place was a mess—plates piled everywhere, glasses stacked and smashed, stale food scattered around—and on a table at the centre of this mess, the reason Jammer had chosen to send me this way.

Fod Larima's head had been turned a rich, bloody red by the oven's heat. His hair was still there, tied up in several bunches to prevent any of it corrupting his meat. His eye sockets were empty, and in his mouth was stuffed a fat truffle. From the neck down to his feet his carcass was stripped bare. Shreds of meat still stained his spine and ribs, but there was very little left.

I stared at him for a few rapid heartbeats, and before leaving I muttered my apology. ⟡